his unfolding plan

EVA WEBSTER

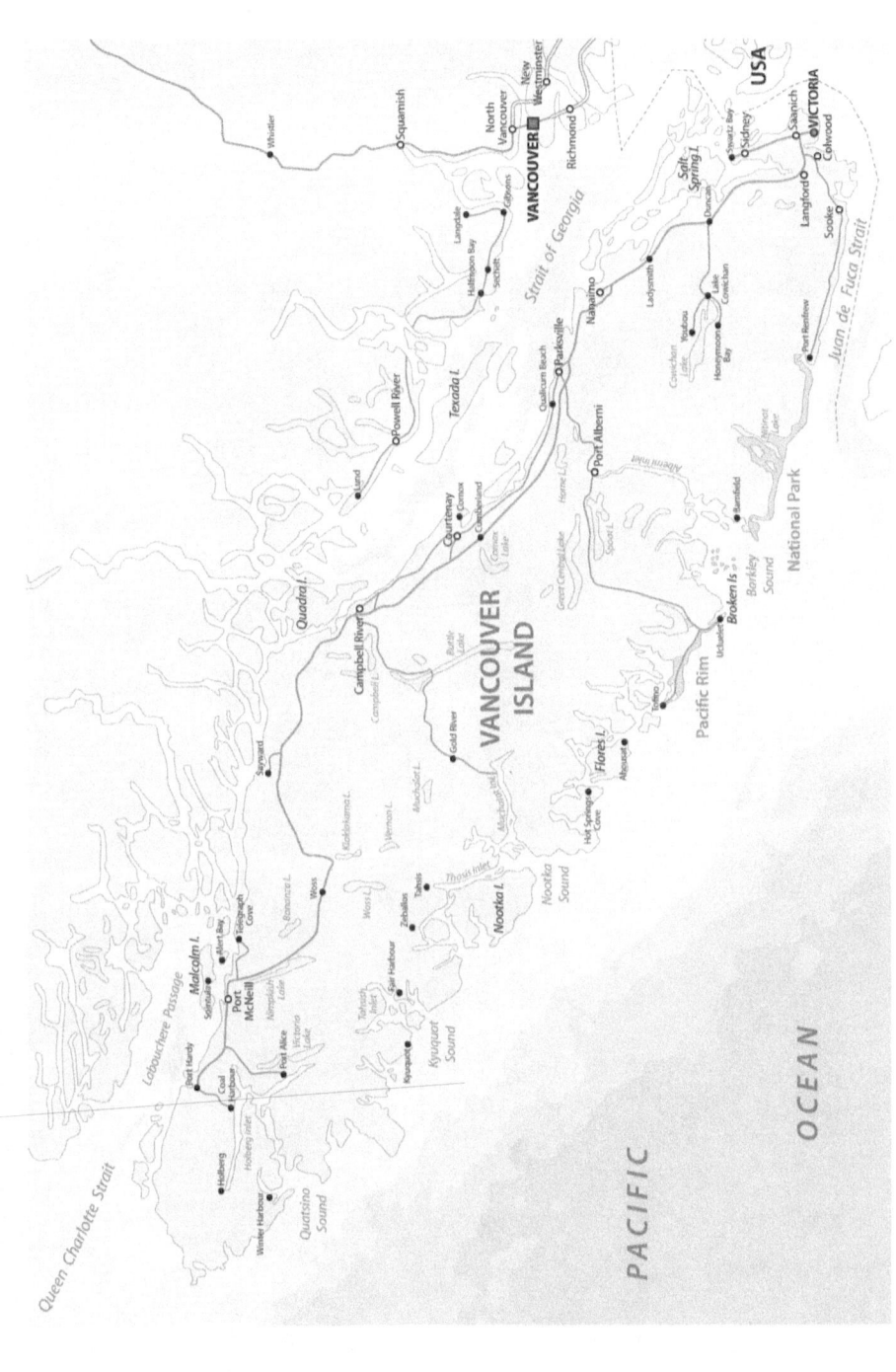

Dedicated to My Loving Heavenly Father, My Lord and Saviour Jesus Christ and the Holy Spirit who lives in me.

Paperback ISBN: 978-1-7380564-0-8

eBook ISBN: 978-1-7380564-1-5

characters

Kate Grayson
twenty-six-year-old teacher

Matt and Becky Grayson
Kate's parents

Lily Grayson
Kate's Grandmother

Mr. Scott
older gentleman

Mrs. Wilson
neighbour

Stuart Coghill
Kate's boyfriend

Joanne and Don Smith

retired missionaries from Papua New Guinea

Sarah Smith

deceased daughter of Joanne and Don

Lily and Al Grayson

Kate's grandparents

Mr. Howet

lawyer for Kate's parents

Martha Weston

nurse for Lily Grayson

Dana Moffet

legal secretary

Paul Moffet

chaplain at Nanaimo Hospital and cousin to Dana

Sandy

housekeeper and cook for Lily Grayson

Bill

groundskeeper for Lily Grayson

Mr. Nottingham

representative of Invasive Species Council of BC

Judy Portus
nurse at McMaster

Jodie
manager of the home for unwed mothers

Officer Hagen
RCMP officer

Mrs. Stevens
Crown Counsel

Bruce McDowell
Doctor at Nanaimo Hospital

Jerry Dunsmore
young man who killed Kate's parents

Dr. Richards
coroner at Nananio Hospital

Greg Daniels
representative of car manufacturer

Garth Ellsworth
Private Investigator

Mike Harding
lawyer and a friend of Paul's

Mr. Baskin

Jerry's lawyer

chapter one

The funeral service was over, and their bodies were buried. At a time when Kate craved seclusion to endure her misery and grief, she saw yet another person approaching her. Mrs. Wilson, an elderly neighbour, made her way slowly across the reception room of the funeral home, intent on speaking with Kate. "It was a lovely service. They certainly honoured your Mother and Father for devoting their lives to helping the less fortunate. I'll miss the chats I had with them each evening when they took a stroll around the neighbourhood."

"It was kind of you to come," Kate said as Mrs. Wilson turned and walked towards the door. At that moment, she wished she could hit a rewind button and return to a life without grief, tears, or unanswered questions.

Kate stared at the funeral home's reception area,

cluttered with empty tea cups and sandwich trays, and she felt the whole day was surreal. This was a nightmare she could never have predicted. Two weeks ago, Kate had said goodbye to her second-grade students for the summer holidays and shut the door to her classroom. Her parents, Matt and Becky Grayson, were taking a trip to Vancouver Island and if she hadn't signed up months earlier for a creative writing course on Children's Literature, she would have accompanied them. The summer spread out before her with dreams of writing and spending time with her boyfriend, Stuart. But now everything has changed. Her plans didn't include the death of the two people she loved most and her writing was put on hold.

Kate suddenly became aware of an overpowering smell of roses and carnations. She could feel herself nearing the breaking point–the point at which you either collapse or frantically search for a way to escape the emptiness, exhaustion and stress that has brought you to this moment. A rising sense of panic gripped her. Kate felt desperate to get home, to a place where she felt safe. She needed the comfort of familiar surroundings. Home would never be the same now, but at least she would be out of the public eye and could mourn the loss of her parents without being told people understood how she was feeling, the Lord had a plan for her, or how time would heal everything. Kate wanted to scream at the people who talked about trivialities, gave her fake hugs and told her they would be there for her. Her church had never been there for her. Although they had attended a large evangelical church for a little over a year, and she and her parents had tried to make friends, people had not invited them into their lives or made any effort to get to know them. Sometimes she thought moving to St. Thomas had been a mistake, but it was where she had been hired for a teaching job. Her parents decided since they were retired, they would join her. Together they built a cozy bungalow in a new subdivision off Sunset Drive. Matt and Becky had enjoyed the slower pace of life in St. Thomas, and she had fulfilled her dream of becoming a teacher. They felt so blessed.

Then, unexpectedly, Kate met Stuart. He knocked on their door one day, two months ago, saying he had clients who wanted to purchase a bungalow like theirs and asked if they would consider selling. They told him they were not interested, but before he left, he asked Kate if she would join him for a coffee. Stuart impressed Kate with his charming manner and good looks. She accepted the invitation with no hesitation. They chatted over their coffee and Stuart shared his goal of opening his own real estate business in the near future. He made a point of telling Kate that many of his clients had been contacts through the church. As it turned out, Kate and her parents attended the same church as Stuart. Over the next few months, they dated regularly.

Kate continued to scan the funeral home's tearoom and saw Stuart in his impeccably tailored suit and silk tie near the door, talking to an elderly, frail-looking

3

gentleman they knew from church. Kate pushed back her chair and quickly covered the distance.

"Excuse me, Mr. Scott, but I need Stuart to get the car and take me home."

"Of course, my dear. You must be worn out. A very hard day for you. My prayers are with you."

"I'll get the car," Stuart mumbled as he pulled the keys out of his pocket and frowned at Kate.

Kate hopped into the Corvette as soon as it pulled up to the ornate front doors of the funeral home.

"I had that old guy almost convinced to sell his house until you appeared and interrupted our conversation. Really, Kate, you need to wait until I finish. I acquire some of my best contacts at social events like this."

"Then I guess you plan on continuing your discussion with him," responded Kate as she quietly wiped away a few tears that had escaped her eyes.

"I'm just dropping you off. Get changed and relax and I'll be back when I can."

The moment the car stopped in front of the small red brick bungalow, Kate opened the door and jumped out. Hardly able to see for tears, she ran to the front door and opened it. Once inside, a tsunami of tears cascaded down her face, marking her dress. Collapsing in her Father's recliner, she sobbed and sobbed until she was so exhausted that she could barely breathe. Kate could finally unleash all the shock and sorrow she had buried for the last two weeks. But why was she alone, with no support? Did Stuart really care about her? Didn't he understand she needed his compassion at a time like this? Oh, how she missed her parents. Her heart was ready to burst with the sorrow of her loss. It wasn't until the service today when the funeral director took her aside and opened the caskets for her private viewing, that she realized they were actually gone. Her life, as she knew it and liked it, would never be the same. She wished she could have told them one more time what wonderful parents they were and how much she loved them. They had provided such unconditional love and were her cheering section, always encouraging her to try her best and not give up.

The chiming of the doorbell interrupted Kate's thoughts. Slowly walking to the door, she turned on the outside light and unlocked it. A lady in her mid-sixties stood there with a casserole and a sympathetic look.

"Hello. You don't know me, but I just heard at a prayer meeting this morning that your parents' funeral was today. I wanted to stop by and tell you how sorry I am for your loss. My name is Joanne Smith. I made our favourite casserole, Hawaiian Beans. It freezes well if you can't use it right now."

"Thank you for your kindness. Please come in and I'll transfer the beans to one of our dishes so you can take this one back home."

Joanne followed Kate to the kitchen, thinking how cozy the room looked with the white cupboards and red gingham curtains and tablecloth. "Kate, you don't have to worry about the dish. There's no rush to get it back to me. My husband and I are staying at a friend's home for a week or so until we find a place to buy or rent. We recently returned from the mission field and hope to retire in this area. "

"Please have a seat," Kate said, as she pointed to the kitchen table. She stood there looking confused. "I'm sorry. I don't know what's wrong with me. For the life of me, I can't remember where Mom kept the casserole dishes."

"What you're experiencing is entirely normal. Right now, your mind and heart are trying to come to grips with the tremendous loss you're feeling. Give yourself some time and things will right themselves, but for now, nothing will seem normal. I had the same experience of not remembering where things were when my daughter died. So please just keep the dish until you have finished the casserole.

"Thank you for being so thoughtful and understanding. You're so easy to talk to and I don't feel I have to keep up some stoic front. I'm a Christian and I know my parents have gone to heaven, so I shouldn't keep feeling like I need to cry."

"My dear girl, Christians have the same feelings of loss and sorrow as everyone else. The only difference is we hope to see our loved ones again and spend all eternity with them. That's a wonderful comfort. But crying is a natural response to grief. Even Jesus cried at Lazarus' tomb. It's much better to let the tears flow and the heart heal. Would you like to tell me what happened to your parents or would you rather I leave you alone? You have had a very stressful day and you must be exhausted."

Sitting down at the kitchen table, Kate sighed and looked over at Mrs. Smith. "Actually, I really appreciate your company. I feel so alone. My boyfriend was supposed to come back for a while, but he chose to work. I was experiencing what I call a meltdown when you knocked on the door. I'm sure my eyes are red and my face is blotchy. To tell you the truth, I don't even care," sniffled Kate "My parents got an unexpected phone call from my Father's Mother, Lily Grayson, who lives in Qualicum Beach on Vancouver Island. My Father's parents disowned him when he became a Christian and decided to attend Bible College. His Father told him that if he wasn't interested in running the family business and was determined to be a religious fanatic, then he could have no further contact with them. Dad tried to reason with them but his Father, in particular, was very stubborn. For the past forty-odd years, Dad has continued to make an effort, but no response. Then three weeks ago, they got a note from my Grandmother saying Dad's Father had died of a heart attack. She wanted my Father and Mother to come to the Island to see her since she hadn't been well for quite some time. They booked a flight and left a few days later. They made it safely to the Island, rented a car at the airport, and were on the Old Island Highway headed to my Grandmother's home. A truck driven by a young man coming in the opposite direction crossed the centre line and crashed into my parents' rental car head-on. My parents were killed. I still feel as though this is a terrible nightmare, and I will wake up to see Mom baking in the kitchen and Dad sitting in his favourite chair reading."

As the tears cascaded down her face again, Joanne reached over and took her hand. "If you love deeply, you will grieve deeply. Eventually, the tears won't come as often and the pain won't feel as intense. I want to share with you just two pieces of advice I was given when I lost my daughter. First, get lots of rest because grief is tiring, and things always look worse when you are tired. Second, don't make any big decisions without praying about it and ensuring it's God's will for your life. I can tell you are the kind of daughter any parent would be proud to have. Your parents raised you in a Christian home, so draw upon what they taught you. Could you give me a piece of paper and a pen? I'll write my name and phone number, so if you need anyone to talk with, call me."

Kate slid a notebook and pen across to Joanne. "Thank you so much for taking the time to come over. I truly felt like I was falling apart. God led you here tonight because he knew I needed support."

As Joanne reached the front door, it opened and Stuart walked in.

"Oh, Mrs. Smith, this is my boyfriend, Stuart. Stuart, Mrs. Smith."

"Nice to meet you, Stuart," Joanne said with a smile.

Something like a grunt came from Stuart, who

continued to walk through the hall and into the kitchen.

"Well, goodbye, Kate. Remember, I'm only a phone call away if you need me."

"Thank you again, Mrs. Smith."

"Please call me Joanne."

Shutting the door, Kate turned back toward the kitchen. Stuart was sitting at the table with a disgruntled look on his face. "So, who was that old girl?"

"Joanne is one of the most kindhearted people I have ever met. Christ's love radiates from her, and I hope she'll become a close friend. Unfortunately, since coming to St. Thomas, I have found it difficult to make friends. I'd hoped the church would be more friendly, but everyone seems to have a little group that I can't break into no matter how pleasant I try to be."

"You know, Kate, not everything has to be about you. When I returned to the funeral home, Mr. Scott was getting into his car and didn't want to discuss selling his home. He said something about speaking with the Lord before speaking any further with me. Some people take their religion too far. But if you hadn't been in such a hurry to get home, I probably would have sweet-talked him into selling."

Kate rubbed her hand over her forehead. "I'm too tired and drained from the funeral to continue this discussion. I'm going to take headache medication and rest. You can let yourself out."

"What? You're not going to warm up this casserole and get us dinner?"

"No, Stuart, I'm not. Goodnight."

With tears once again streaming down her cheeks, Kate shut her bedroom door and headed for the medicine chest. She stole a quick glance in the mirror and was shocked at what a wreck she was. Her eyes were bloodshot and puffy, and her makeup was smeared. No wonder Stuart was treating her like an old dishcloth. That was what she looked like. Discarding her clothes over a chair, Kate grabbed her pyjamas, and in no time, found herself lying in bed. She felt so alone. No one from her Bible Study Group or the Book Club at church had come to the funeral to support her. Just a few elderly people who had spoken to her and her parents had bothered to interrupt their lives to comfort her. A few close friends from Burlington, where they had lived for many years, had made the two-hour trip to the funeral. It was so good to see them.

But Stuart had been a disappointment. Kate was sure she had found the man of her dreams. But lately, she was seeing another side to him that didn't fit with what she wanted in a husband. Aside from the hug he had given her the night her parents died, he had spent very little time with her, claiming summer was his busiest time of the year since the housing market was so hot. It also puzzled her why Stuart never came to the door to pick her up for a date. He always called on his cell phone when he was nearly there and asked her to meet him outside. Kate realized she did not understand some of Stuart's behaviours. Spotting her Bible lying on the nightstand, Kate turned to her Mother's favourite verse, Romans 8:28, 'And we know that all things work together for good to them that love God, to them who are the called according to his purpose.'

"Lord, I need your help, as I've never needed it before. I feel unloved and alone. I know you're with me, so help me cling to that truth. You understand my sorrow, and I need your comfort. I'm so disappointed in people who've let me down, but you never disappoint me. Help me make my life count for you, and give me the wisdom to know what you want me to do. Thank you for giving me two such amazing parents. I know they're safe in your care, but I miss them so much it hurts. I could always depend on them, and now it seems like there is no one. Thank you for bringing Joanne here today. Please help me sleep and face tomorrow. In Christ's name. Amen."

chapter two

With the sun streaming through her window, Kate grabbed her housecoat and headed to the kitchen. Her headache had left, but she still didn't feel hungry. Her heart was so full of grief and sorrow that she couldn't feel any hunger pains. She knew if her Mother was there, she would insist Kate eat breakfast. The memory of all those happy mornings the three of them spent around the breakfast table, feasting on her Mother's delicious meals, brought unbidden tears to her eyes. She still expected her Dad to come through the door, lured by the smell of bacon frying to ask if breakfast was ready. She plugged in the toaster and coffee maker, and sat down to think about what she should do today. Truth be told, she didn't feel like doing anything today but climbing back into bed and waiting for this nightmare to pass. The sound of the toast popping up and the smell of coffee brought her back to the present.

Bowing her head to thank the Lord for her food, she asked Him to direct her steps and give her wisdom in deciding what to do next.

As Kate walked over to the sink to rinse her dishes and place them in the dishwasher, she glanced out the window over her Father's manicured gardens and realised she needed to cut the grass. She assisted her Father in the spring with planting the flowers. During her holidays, she cut the grass. But he was the master gardener and loved everything about his garden. The ringing of the phone interrupted another precious memory.

"Hello."

"Kate, is that you, dear? It's your Grandmother speaking."

"Yes."

"I tried to get you last night, but no one answered. I wish my health was better so I could have been there for the funeral. To think I came so close to seeing your Father after so many years and meeting your Mother for the first time. This terrible accident happened as they were only five miles from my home."

"We buried them yesterday, but I miss them more than words can ever say."

"Dear, I don't know how you'll feel about this, but I'd like to have you come out here for the rest of the summer. I've never met you, Kate. I know that was our fault, but before my life on this earth comes to an end, I'd love to have spent some time with my only Granddaughter. What do you think?"

"I'm finding it hard to concentrate and make decisions. I'll have to pray about it."

"Thank you, Kate, for even considering a visit."

"Goodbye."

As Kate hung up the phone, she could feel a surge of anger. If her Grandparents hadn't treated her Father so severely when he was young, she'd have grown up knowing them. Her parents wouldn't have been killed on the Island Highway going to see her grandmother at her invitation. What kind of a woman would disown her son? She had hurt her Father deeply, and now she wanted her to uproot her life and pay a visit. Maybe it was time Grandmother got a little of her own medicine.

Within the hour, Kate was dressed in her jeans and had the lawnmower ready to go. She was about to yank the cord to start it when she suddenly remembered she had a meeting with the lawyer at eleven o'clock. She had been forgetting so many things lately. Kate had about an hour and a half to get the lawn cut and get over there. She paused as she heard a car come up the gravel on the driveway. As Kate pushed the lawnmower to the front of the house, she recognized Joanne accompanied by a gray-haired, pleasant-looking man.

"Kate, I want you to meet my husband, Don."

"Hello, Don," Kate said, as she shook his outstretched hand.

"Nice to meet you. My wife said she had a lovely visit with you yesterday. Joanne insisted we come this morning and see if we could be of any help. We need to look for a place to rent this afternoon but our morning is free.

"If you could cut the grass, I'd appreciate it. Unfortunately, I forgot about an appointment with the lawyer. I don't know exactly what he wants, but I need to be there by eleven."

"Why don't I pull a few weeds from the gardens while Don is cutting the grass? We both love gardening."

"Great. The gardening gloves and a small hoe and any other tools are in Dad's tool shed. I'll leave the back door unlocked, and you can go in and have some of the casserole you brought me yesterday. I didn't eat any last night because I had a frightful headache so I don't want it to go to waste. There's coffee made on the counter."

"Don't worry about a thing, dear."

The Smiths had no sooner headed to the backyard when Stuart pulled up. Impeccably groomed as usual, he greeted her with a warm hug.

"Are you feeling better, Kate?"

It felt so good to have someone put their arms around her and make her feel cared for.

"Yes, my headache is gone and I'm off to see Mr. Howet, our lawyer. Do you want a cup of coffee before I go, or do you have houses to show this morning?"

"Only one house to show in half an hour. I could use a cup of coffee."

"I'll get changed while you pour us both one."

Kate looked stunning as she returned to the kitchen, dressed in beige linen pants with a matching jacket, her auburn hair falling softly around her shoulders.

"Your coffee is on the table. Just the way you like it," Stuart said as he pointed to the table from the counter where he was looking out over the backyard.

Stuart was so warm and caring today, nothing like yesterday. Maybe she was so upset yesterday that she hadn't reacted well to people. She'd always been too sensitive. Anyway, Kate liked the Stuart she was with today.

"So why does the lawyer need to see you?"

"I'm not sure. I know my parents left me the house and any money they had saved. Dad never had a high-paying job, so I'm sure there wasn't a lot. When Mr. Howet attended the funeral service yesterday, he said he'd seen the death notice in the paper, and he asked me to meet him at his office today. So I guess I'll find out at eleven o'clock."

Putting their cups in the sink, they went out the back door to their cars.

"Call me when you get back from the lawyer's office. I noticed you didn't lock the back door after you got outside."

"I'm leaving it open for the Smiths. Remember Joanne, who brought me the casserole? She and her husband came over this morning and kindly offered to help me by doing some gardening-related chores."

"You just met that woman yesterday, and you're giving them free run of the house. Are you crazy?"

The Stuart from yesterday was returning. With tears in her eyes, Kate got into her Honda Civic and backed up, leaving Stuart with another disgruntled look on his face.

Driving down Sunset Drive, she stopped at the cemetery. The gates were open so she drove through to her parents' graves. She parked right in front of them and walked over the dew-covered grass to where the soil was disturbed. The funeral director left the massive wreath of carnations she had bought on top of the graves.

"I miss you so much. Our home is not the same. You encouraged me through all the difficult times. I know you're safe in heaven with the Lord, but my world isn't the same without you. Did you like Stuart? You never said what you thought of him. I'm totally confused about my feelings right now. You both will live in my heart and my memories forever. Thank you for loving me and for all the sacrifices you made to educate me. I'll be back. I love you."

Wiping the tears from her eyes, Kate started her car and continued down Sunset Drive to the lawyer's office. Mr. Howet's cute young receptionist asked her to have a seat since he was just finishing up with another client. She chose a comfortable leather armchair and tried to relax. She was admiring the beautiful pictures of wild animals decorating the walls when the door opened and Stuart walked in.

"The couple I'm meeting texted me to say they were

running late, so I'll have time to be present when you meet the lawyer."

"How did you know where to come?"

"Kate, your memory has been terrible the last couple of weeks. You told me the name of your lawyer this morning, so I googled it on my phone and got his address. You really need to snap out of your daydreaming and get back into the real world."

"This is a very difficult time for me, so please cut me some slack."

"We need to plan our future, Kate, not stay in the past."

A door leading from Mr. Howet's office opened. He escorted his client out and turned with a smile to address Kate. "Hello. You had a lovely service for your parents yesterday. Your Father's friend, Rev. McNalley, preached a comforting sermon with a personal touch. You could tell that he knew how dedicated your Father was to helping others. I'm sorry for the rush in meeting with you, but I'll explain in my office."

"Mr. Howet, this is my boyfriend, Stuart Coghill. The men shook hands and Mr. Howet took Kate's elbow to lead her into his office. Stuart followed. At the door, Mr. Howet turned to Stuart.

"I'll have to ask you to wait for Kate in the waiting room, Mr. Coghill."

"But I'm here to support her."

"That's very commendable, but friends don't have legal rights. If she needs your support, I'll come and get you."

Mr. Howet closed the door to his office and asked Kate to have a seat.

"Kate, you must be wondering why I refused to let Stuart come in. Let me explain. Over the years, I've been the lawyer for many women who have inherited property from their parents or husbands. When a male arrives at my office who is not legally married to them, I'm concerned about the kind of pressure these men can exert while they are vulnerable. Sometimes they appear to be caring and fill a loneliness gap. But what they really want is part or all of the inheritance as payment for their support. It isn't that they care about anyone but themselves. Your young man might be a genuinely wonderful fellow. I hope that's the case. But please don't rush into any decisions right now. If you love someone, there is no rush. If they love you, you will not feel pressured into doing anything. Your parents requested I speak with you about their will in private. I'm honouring their wishes as well. If you want me to include Stuart at another time, that will be up to you."

"I understand, Mr. Howet."

"I'm sure you wonder why I've asked you to come so soon after the funeral. Again, I'm doing this at your parents' request. They wanted to put your mind at ease about funeral expenses and what they have left you. Firstly, your parents paid for their funerals when they arrived in St. Thomas. You might owe the funeral home a small amount for incidental things, or the light luncheon that you arranged after the funeral, but I have a copy of the receipt for all the money they paid to the funeral home. If they give you a bill that sounds unreasonable, please let me see it before you pay. I don't think anyone will try to take advantage of you, but you are grieving and vulnerable, so it is best to be wary."

Once more, Kate was aware of how her parents had taken steps to protect her. Trying not to break into sobs, Kate nodded and swallowed the lump in her throat.

"Now, as for the will, Kate, your parents left you their savings and the house as well as any material possessions they accumulated. They did, however, put some conditions or restraints in place. These are for your protection. They didn't put them in place because they didn't trust your judgement or felt that you were irresponsible. On the contrary, your parents felt you were the best gift God had ever given them. Everything they have done has been to prevent anyone from pressuring you into doing something you don't want to do. You can't sell the house for a year, although you are at liberty to rent it if you don't want to live there. Their modest savings are to be left as they are for a year and then they will be yours to do with as you want. Your parents, as you know, did not believe in having debt, so you do not require any money to pay off loans etc. When the time comes, I'll give the bank a document signed by them and a copy of their will, making this transfer possible."

The tears, which Kate fought to control, now flowed freely. "I'm so sorry about being emotional. I'm overwhelmed by the way they've taken steps to protect me. I'd much rather have them here with me, alive and well, than all the money in the world. It's all so empty without them."

"I only met your parents a few weeks ago when they came in to discuss their will and draft up this other document. They were concerned about travelling and wanted to make sure there were no loose ends before they left. I've never met two more caring and sincere people. Your Father told me they had started a street mission in Hamilton."

"Yes, they'd say they worked for the Lord. They were always helping people. Mom and Dad wouldn't have been considered successful by the world's standards, but today in heaven, I know they're being rewarded."

"Your parents asked me to give you this envelope if anything were to happen to them. I believe it's a letter written to you about three weeks ago. If I can help you with anything, or if anyone tries to pressure you into any business ventures, don't hesitate to call and ask my receptionist for an appointment immediately. I have a daughter in university, just a few years younger than you, and I'd like to think she had someone to turn to if anything happened to my wife and me."

"Thank you, Mr. Howet. I'll just try to deal with one day at a time until life seems more normal."

Picking up the envelope, Kate quietly walked to the door. Stuart was nowhere to be seen. She approached the young receptionist. "Could you tell me if Stuart left?"

"Yes," Dana replied. "He didn't like Mr. Howet telling him he couldn't accompany you inside the office and he stormed out."

Kate, disappointed once again by Stuart, headed out to her car. Turning the key, she expected to hear it start but nothing happened. Not another problem. After the third try, she knew something was definitely wrong. Her car had never let her down before. She grabbed her purse and searched for her cell phone. No cell phone. Then Kate remembered she had put it on the kitchen counter to recharge last night. She would have to go back into the office and call CAA. Just as she started back towards the building, Dana emerged, walking towards the parking lot.

"Kate, did you forget something ?"

"I don't know where my brain is these days. I seem to be in some kind of fog. The car won't start, and I came out without my cell phone. I wonder what else I have forgotten to do. I'm usually very organized."

"It's just part of grief. Life will return to normal at some point, but don't be too hard on yourself right now. I have my cell phone. Are you a member of the CAA?"

"Oh, yes. Dad insisted that I be able to get help."

Using Dana's phone, Kate put through her call and was assured a tow truck would be out shortly.

"Thank you so much," Kate said with a tremble in her voice and eyes full of unshed tears.

"Glad to be of help. I'll wait with you until the truck comes. They are usually fast in St. Thomas."

As they waited beside Kate's car, Dana gave Kate time to compose herself by chatting and sharing a few things. "I've been where you are right now, Kate. My parents died within six months of each other from cancer. Like you, I have no siblings, just a cousin who lives on Vancouver Island. I try to keep in touch with him, but life is busy and we don't talk as much as we should. I started working for Mr. Howet about eight months ago, after completing a legal secretarial course. I find it fascinating and I've toyed with the idea of going back to university part-time to become a lawyer. Doesn't that sound crazy?"

"No, we need more women in the legal field. I think you should at least give it a try. Better to do it now before you have other commitments. I'm so glad I completed my education before anything happened to Mom and Dad."

"Well, thanks for the encouragement, Kate."

Suddenly, a red and yellow tow truck with CAA written on the side pulled into the parking lot. The young man smiled and asked Kate for her CAA card and her keys. After jotting down her information on a clipboard, he slid into her car and tried to start it. Again nothing happened.

"I see what your problem is," he announced with a grin as he exited the car. "You're out of gas. Fortunately, I always bring a container with me because this has happened more times than I can count. I'll have you on your way in about two minutes."

"How could I have forgotten to fill up with gas?" moaned Kate.

"You have all kinds of things on your mind right now, and a lot of decisions to make, so it's only natural that you're going to feel overwhelmed," Dana said.

As the CAA truck drove off, Kate turned to Dana. "Thank you so much for your kindness. I felt kind of stranded. Would you be able to come over for lunch someday?"

"I never turn down a meal. Just give me a call at the office."

After stopping to fill the car up with gas, Kate headed home. As she walked up the stone path leading to the front door, she noticed how neat the lawn and gardens looked after the Smiths had finished cutting the grass and weeding. They were the kind of Christians who saw a need and did something positive to help. Her parents had been like that. Leaving her purse and keys on the ledge inside the front door, Kate walked through to the kitchen, where a delicious smell was coming from the oven. On the table was a brief note from Joanne.

Hi Kate,

Finished the yard work and we are off to look at rentals. Left the casserole in the oven for you. Even if you aren't starving, eat a little, at least. I'm sure it'll help you feel a bit better.

24

If you need me, just give me a call.
Joanne

If the old saying is true that every cloud has a silver lining, then this dear couple was her silver lining. Taking a small china dish out of the cupboard, Kate opened the oven and removed the casserole. She suddenly remembered that she should change her clothes in case she was sloppy. But the bean casserole smelled so tempting, she decided to risk it. Kate was enjoying it when the phone rang.

"Hello."

"I have some exciting news. I'll be over shortly," Stuart announced.

He hung up before Kate could say anything else. Putting the dishes in the dishwasher, she wondered what the exciting news could be. Stuart certainly sounded cheerful. She hoped the good news didn't involve going back out since she was ready for a quiet afternoon and time alone to read her parents' letter.

The doorbell announced Stuart's arrival. He was carrying his briefcase and certainly looked pleased about something.

"After I showed a client a house this morning, I had time to look up some info on homes on your street that've sold recently, and you'll get an extremely good price if you list it right now. There's a shortage of bungalows for sale and people are moving out of the crowded cities and looking to retire here. With what you get for this house, you can invest in the realty business that I want to open. We could be partners. I took the time to write up a contract for you, and I have a sign to put on your front lawn. I'll take care of everything, and you have nothing to do but keep the house tidy for my showings."

"Stuart, it's too soon for me to make any decisions. Right now, this house is a comfort to me. I can see my Mom puttering around inside, and Dad in his flannel shirt and blue jeans doing the gardening. I feel their presence here. I'm an emotional wreck at the moment and I can't make any big decisions. Anyway, my parents set up the will so I couldn't sell the house, or use the money in their bank accounts for a year.

"Maybe they stashed some money in the house. Lots of seniors don't trust the banks and keep a nest egg at home."

"My Dad didn't have a high-paying job, and my university education and Teachers' College were costly, and I know they made many sacrifices. This trip to British Columbia was the first trip I ever remember them planning. They were not financially well off and I'm sure they didn't have money hidden in the house. I'm sorry to disappoint you but that's the situation. Would you like some of the casserole? There's enough left for both of us."

Stuart jammed the contract into his briefcase and scowled. "I've obviously wasted a good portion of my morning. I have work back at the office and calls to return. I think I misjudged the situation here. Call me when, and if, you find a way to cooperate with my plans." Turning, he stormed out the door, leaving it to bang and shake the house.

What had just happened? If Kate understood what Stuart had just said correctly, it looked like their relationship was over. He'd been so attentive and pleasant when they started dating, but as time went on, more demanding and controlling. Fortunately, her parents encouraged her from childhood to think for herself and pray about everything. So, bowing her head and with more tears coursing down her cheeks, Kate did just that.

"Lord, I feel so alone. As if losing my parents isn't bad enough, I don't like the way Stuart is treating me. I thought he was going to be the one. What should I do? I feel so angry and I know that isn't right. I'm angry at my parents for going on this trip. I'm angry at Stuart for not understanding the support I need, and at my church for not caring. I know you're with me, but sometimes I feel I lack a person here on earth who cares, really cares. Thank you for listening and helping me to be the person you want me to be."

Suddenly, Kate remembered the envelope containing the letter from her parents. Now, where had she put it? Probably, it was still in her purse. As she entered the living room, she saw her purse on the shelf inside the front door, where she had thrown it upon returning from the lawyer's office. The letter was sticking out of the zippered compartment on the front. Grabbing it, she hurried back to the living room and curled up on the sofa.

Dearest Kate,

If you're reading this letter, then something has happened to both your Father and me. I can only imagine how hard this is for you. How I wish I could put my arms around you.

We waited for many years before you came into our lives as a gift from God. We couldn't have asked for a more loving and caring daughter. You brought joy and laughter into our home, and raising you to love the Lord has been the greatest privilege of our lives. We saw you unfold like a rosebud coming into bloom. Your talents in sewing and teaching have been observable to all. Your kindness to people and your love for animals, particularly rescue dogs, has helped so many.

This trip to connect with your Grandmother is one that we feel the Lord wants us to make. I have never met her and your Father hasn't had an interaction with his parents since university. He has tried many times to contact them, but they refused to respond. I know that hurt him deeply. When we got word, a week ago, that his Father had died and his Mother wanted us to visit, we prayed about it and decided this was a door God had opened. We don't know how this visit will go, but we'll leave that in the Lord's hands.

Now for some words of wisdom. Kate, people will fail you, but the Lord never will. When you are hurt, forgive, pray for the person who hurt you, and move on. If you don't forgive, bitterness will affect all your relationships. Next, don't live in the past. Life is about change and. moving ahead. God might direct you to be a teacher for many years or he might have another plan. Don't be afraid to go where he leads. Look to him for strength to tackle any challenge. At some point in your life, you might think you have met your soulmate. Beauty fades over time, but character remains. How that person treats you and others is an indication of what they are made of. Foremost, this person needs to know Christ and live for him. Just because someone goes to church does not mean they are a Christian. So please do not rush into marriage, but give yourself time to see what the person is really like. Anyone can be on their best behaviour for a short time, but eventually, you will see the real person. There is so much more I could say, but if you pray about everything, the Lord will guide you.

I never want you to think that you didn't have a chance to say goodbye or tell us that you loved us. We know you love us from the way you showed your love. Actions always speak louder than words. Second, there is no need to say goodbye to Christians. We will meet again in Heaven.

We are no longer physically with you, but we are in your heart and your memories. Someday we'll be together again. The Bible describes Heaven, our eternal home, and I have always thought how splendid it will be. No sickness, no sorrow, no problems of any kind. Try to be happy for us. Yes, mourn for a time but don't stay there. Your love for the past twenty-six years has been a blessing straight from the hand of God. You will always be our little angel.

Love always.

Mom and Dad

29

Kate finished reading the letter, her progress impeded by tears which had flowed steadily as she was reading and blurred the words. She felt like her parents had given her something precious. There were so many parts of this letter that touched her heart and gave her a feeling of peace in the midst of this horrible time. Kate walked over to her Bible and slipped the letter inside. Next to her Bible, it was the most valuable thing she owned.

The emotional turmoil she had been through exhausted her. A quick nap was appealing, so she spread out on the sofa, grabbed the quilt from behind it and slept peacefully for the first time in over a week.

chapter three

Several hours later, Kate awoke to her cell phone ringing. She swung her legs over the sofa and reached for it on the coffee table. The call display showed a name that she didn't recognize. Still somewhat groggy, she answered.

"Hello."

"Is this Miss Grayson, Kate Grayson?"

"Yes, it is."

"I'm Martha Weston, your Grandmother's nurse. She doesn't know I'm calling. Could I have a few minutes of your time?"

"I have a few minutes," answered Kate hesitantly, still groggy from her sleep and wondering why she was calling.

"Your Grandmother has had a rough couple of weeks, losing first her husband and then her son. She wasn't well before this all happened, but now she seems to have given up. She eats very little and won't even leave the house to sit outside. Her medical issues are also worse. I probably shouldn't have bothered you, but if you could reach out to her, it might help her take an interest in living again."

"I'll have to think this over. I've never met my Grandmother. That was her choice, not mine. For years, my parents tried to reconcile with my grandparents and bring me to meet them, but she and my grandfather did not respond," Kate explained.

"I think she's feeling responsible for your parents' deaths since it was at her invitation they were coming," added Martha.

"As I said, Martha, I'll have to think about it. I'm sure you mean well, but right now, I'm trying to come to terms with my loss."

"Thank you for at least listening to my concerns. Your Grandmother is in failing health, and I felt it was only fair to give you the opportunity to help.

"Thank you, Martha. Goodbye."

She would agree that her Grandmother shared the guilt for her parents being on the Island and, consequently, their death. The thought of going off to a strange place to meet her Grandmother when she had never flown before terrified her. If her Grandparents had wanted nothing to do with her father after he became a Christian, then there was a good chance she wouldn't like Kate either and the trip would be for nothing. Also, as bills had come in during the last few days, Kate realized she would be paying for everything by herself, whereas, before her parents' deaths, they had shared in the expenses. Could she afford to spend the money on a trip to Vancouver Island? It was another decision Kate had to make, but she felt like that part of her brain was frozen and all she could see were the problems.

Thinking that a cup of coffee might revive her, Kate headed for the kitchen. Seeing her notebook on the counter reminded her of Joanne's offer to be available if she needed someone to talk to. Pulling her cell phone from her pocket, she hit her number. Joanne picked up immediately.

"Joanne, it's Kate. I hope I didn't get you at a bad time."

"Not at all, dear. Don and I were just talking about taking a stroll and we thought we might go past your place. Don was going to offer to deadhead some flowers in your garden for you."

"That'd be great, Joanne. I haven't been out there to do a thing. I'm calling because I would really like it if you could sit down with me for a chat. I'm trying to make a decision and I'm finding it so difficult."

"We'll be over shortly, dear."

Kate went outside and removed the lock on the toolshed door so Don would have easy access. Within fifteen minutes, there was a knock on the front door. Joanne was standing there with a plate of sandwiches and a bag of lemon cookies.

"Don has gone directly to the garden to get started," explained Joanne as she followed Kate to the kitchen. "I thought you might enjoy a sandwich and some of my lemon cookies. We had just finished eating when you called."

"Thank you. You are so thoughtful. Have a seat and I'll get us both a cup of coffee.

As you know, my parents were on their way to see my Grandmother when they were killed. I had a call from my Grandmother, the day after the funeral, asking me to come and visit her. I've been very angry since my parents' deaths, and I partially blame my Grandmother for them being on the Island. I didn't tell her I'd come. Then this morning, her nurse called me and said my Grandmother is failing and seems to have given up. She felt that if I involved myself in her life, it might help. I didn't make any commitment to doing so. I can think of several logical reasons for not getting involved. I just don't know what to do."

"Let's pray about this situation and ask for God's guidance, Kate, before we discuss it any further." Bowing their heads, Joanne prayed God would heal the hurt in Kate's heart and help her through this time of sorrow. She also asked that He give them wisdom and direct Kate's path as she made decisions.

"Thank you for praying. I can't even seem to talk to God like I used to. To tell you the truth, I've been angry with him too. There is so much anger in me towards my Grandparents, the Lord, the man who caused my parents' deaths, my church and Stuart. I think I've always had a problem with anger. I find it hard to forgive, and I keep rehearsing the hurts caused by others, and that seems to fuel the anger inside all over again."

"As Christ has forgiven us, he has commanded us to forgive others. That is only fair," Joanne said.

"My Mother and Father left a letter for me with my lawyer. They wrote much the same thing in the letter. And over the years, I've seen them forgive hurts caused by others and treat them with love. My Father was deeply hurt by his parents, but he continually tried to contact them. Even though every attempt failed, he still was prepared to see my Grandmother when she reached out. I need to ask God to forgive my anger and then forgive all the people that I've been angry at, and believe me, there are quite a few. I'm so far from perfect, yet I expect other people to be perfect."

"Anger is usually fueled by unmet expectations," explained Joanne. "In that respect, it is selfish. If someone doesn't do or say what we want them to, then our expectations aren't met and we're angry. No matter how justified we think our anger is, it affects us as a person and hurts our relationship with God."

Grabbing Joanne's hands in her own, Kate thanked Joanne for listening and sharing her heart with her. "I'll be praying and reading the Bible. With God's help, I'll forgive and not let anger have such a hold on my life."

Hearing a knock on the back door, the ladies looked up to see Don entering. "Well, ladies, I think I have the garden looking better. It feels great to be working in one again. We should probably leave shortly as we have an appointment to see an apartment on Scott

Street. It looks like house prices are too high for us, so we're looking for an apartment. Our friends, Beth and Charlie Hunter, have been kind enough to let us stay with them, but they have family coming in a couple of weeks to spend the summer, and we want to find a place before then."

"I'll keep my ears open and if I hear of anything, I'll let you know. Thank you for coming and I thank the Lord for bringing you into my life."

After they left, Kate spent time in prayer and reading her Bible. Her parents' letter was in it and as she reread it, she knew what she had to do. Kate was cleaning up the dishes from the delicious sandwiches and lemon cookies when the phone rang.

"Hi, Kate. It's Dana speaking. I just finished my lunch and I thought I'd give you a call to see how you're doing."

Kate had to think for a moment, trying to remember who Dana was. Then, suddenly, a mental picture of the short young woman with curly blond hair and beautiful turquoise eyes, who was the legal secretary for Mr. Howet, came to mind.

"Hello, Dana. It's great to hear from you. I'm doing okay. I heard from my Grandmother and I think I might fly to Vancouver Island and visit her. I don't know how long I'll be gone. I've never flown before and that terrifies me."

"My cousin Paul lives near Qualicum Beach on the

Island. He's a pastor and the chaplain at the hospital. Every Christmas, when I get a card from him, he asks me to come for a visit. I've always meant to go, but so far, I haven't made the effort. This just gave me an idea. I have holiday time coming. How about we travel together? When were you planning to go?"

"Well, apparently, my Grandmother isn't well, so I think it should be sooner rather than later. I'd like to leave on Friday. I thought I'd book a flight through WestJet from London Airport."

"Can you hold on a minute? Mr. Howet just got back from court, so before he sees his first client for the afternoon, I'll ask him if it's convenient for me to take next week off."

Within a few minutes, Dana was back on the phone and confirmed that the trip was on. She offered to book the flight on Friday from London to Comox on Vancouver Island. From there, they agreed to rent a car, so she offered to book that as well.

Kate, once again, bowed her head and thanked the Lord for providing a travel companion for her. She realized she had a hundred and one things to do before Friday and only three days to get it done. Not knowing how long she would be gone was a concern. Who would check on the house? Her neighbours were mostly young couples who lived an active life, and Kate didn't like to ask them to come over and check on the property. Then another idea seems to be planted in her mind.

She hit Joanne's number. It kept ringing, but no one

was picking up. Just as she was about to hang up, she heard Joanne's voice.

"Joanne, are you back from touring the apartment?"

"Yes, but it turned out to be badly in need of repairs, and the superintendent said that we'd have to make any changes at our own expense. So we'll have to pray about it."

"I have an idea I want to run by you. I feel I should go out to the Island and see my Grandmother. I also want closure about how my parents died. Where did it happen and what was the cause? Knowing this won't bring them back, but it might help me understand. I wondered if you and Don could move into my guest bedroom and look after the house for me. I wish I could tell you how long I'll be gone, but right now I don't know. Even if I end up coming back after a week, you're welcome to stay with me until you find exactly what you need. Would you consider this, or am I asking too much?"

"Can you hold on a moment while I share this with Don?"

"Sure. Please don't feel pressured if this is something that you'd rather not do."

"Don feels this solves both of our problems, so by all means, we take you up on your offer. If you are leaving on Friday, could we move in on Thursday, so you can show us what you need us to do, and get familiar with where things are located. Then on Friday, we can drive you to the airport."

"Sounds like a plan," Kate agreed. "I'm going with

a friend, and she'll be driving us to the airport and parking there. Dana needs to be back in a week. I can stay longer, but that'll depend on how things work out on the Island."

"God seems to be unfolding his plan for both of us. See you on Thursday, Kate."

After hanging up, Kate started making a list of all the things that she needed to accomplish by Friday. For the next two days, she was so busy packing and cleaning that she had very little time for sitting around crying. Although she missed her parents beyond words, she somehow knew they'd approve of her plans. More importantly, as she read her Bible and prayed, she felt assured that God was directing his plan for her life.

chapter four

Friday morning, as Kate and Dana waited at the airport, her cell phone rang. She saw Stuart's number on the screen and hesitated about answering. It had been a week since he huffed out of her house, and in that time she had put a lot of thought into her concept of what her prince charming should be like.

Her anger towards Stuart was gone, and she had forgiven him for his lack of compassion, and for being self-centred with his own plans. Kate knew, however, that she didn't want this relationship to continue. She had to make him understand this was best for both of them.. Answering his call would give her the opportunity to end the relationship. She cringed as she heard his voice.

"Kate, Stuart here. How are you?"

"I'm fine."

"I was thinking of popping in to see you after I

40

show a property on your street today. Now that you have had time to process my offer, we could discuss it in a logical way."

"Well, Stuart, I'm leaving on a trip to Vancouver Island in a few minutes, so you won't find me at home. Our relationship was not meeting either one of our needs, so we're better off ending it. There's no point in having further contact. Take care, Stuart. I wish you all the best as you pursue your dream."

"Why are you going to Vancouver Island?"

"I have to go, Stuart, our plane is loading. Bye."

Gathering their carry-on bags, the two young women handed in their tickets and boarded the plane. Once they were safely airborne, Dana asked Kate about Stuart. "I couldn't help but overhear your conversation with Stuart at the airport. Have you totally broken off or is it on temporary hold?"

"No. I can't speak for Stuart, but it is totally over for me. I should've seen red flags weeks ago, but I convinced myself that I was so blessed to have such a good-looking guy interested in me, I wasn't considering more important aspects, particularly his character. I should've prayed about the relationship as well. I certainly wasn't wise in my decision, but I thought I knew the path my life should take, so I forged ahead with rose-coloured glasses and didn't see what was wrong. I think my parents were aware of the problems ahead, although they never spoke one word against Stuart. When Mr. Howet read me the will, I knew they were protecting me. In their letter, I could read between the lines and sense their concerns. I can't believe I was so foolish."

"We all make mistakes and are works in progress. You've learned a lot from this experience that will help you with the choices you make in the future. And if you keep praying about your choices, you'll get the direction you need. When did Stuart start to become controlling?"

"It happened gradually," Kate explained. "But after my parents died, it escalated, and he didn't hesitate to let me know I wasn't cooperating with his plans."

"He probably thought you'd be desperate to have someone in your life, so he no longer had to be charming. Some women put up with that kind of treatment, but I'm not one of them. Sure, I'd like to meet someone who loves the Lord. But if he doesn't care about my needs as much as his own, it's a deal breaker. So far, I haven't found my soulmate. Changing the subject, I'm really glad your Grandmother invited me to stay at her home with you. The last time Paul asked me to visit, his parents were both alive, so it was certainly okay to stay at their house. But now that he lives there alone, it doesn't seem like the proper thing for a single female and single male to be living in the house without others there. Many people would see that as an archaic concept, but that was how I was brought up."

"Yes. That was what my parents taught me, too. I don't think I could've agreed to stay at Grandmother's place if you weren't coming with me, because I honestly don't know what to expect. Our conversation on the phone lasted only a couple of minutes. We're total strangers. So we might find ourselves hopping back in the car and looking for other accommodation. I've prayed about it and I'll leave it in the Lord's hands."

For the first few hours, the two friends spent their time chatting and getting better acquainted. Dana shared her passion for sketching, and Kate elaborated on her goal of writing a book for children. They both liked gospel music, reading and trying new crafts. They didn't go to the same church, but they both knew the Lord, and that made for an even stronger bond.

Suddenly, the flat land below changed and a vast mountain range loomed in the distance. Kate, who sat in the window seat, and had a bird's view of what was ahead, could hardly contain her excitement. As they got closer, the sheer majesty of the snow-capped mountains, and the abundant forests covering the sides of the mountains were breathtaking.

"I had no idea of the magnitude and beauty of the Canadian Rockies," Kate commented. "I wonder if you can see them from Vancouver Island."

"We'll be there soon and you'll see for yourself," Dana said. "I'm guessing that anything that immense can be seen from a long distance."

Within the hour, they landed at Comox Airport, collected their luggage, made their way to the car-rental desk and loaded their bags into the silver sedan. Then, armed with the map and the GPS on their smartphones, they started along the Old Island Highway."

"You can smell the salty ocean air, and once in a while, I notice a floral-like fragrance probably coming from flowers growing along the road," Dana said as she pointed to a clump of bushes out in bloom.

"I wish I knew where my parents were killed on this highway. While I'm here, I intend to get answers to questions about their deaths."

"Maybe your grandmother can answer them, but we can investigate on our own if she can't. I don't blame you for wanting to know."

The drive along the Old Island Highway turned out to be fascinating, and the scenery was so breathtaking that the girls enjoyed the drive for many miles with no conversation. After cruising along for about an hour, they passed the small hamlet of Bowser.

"Dana, do you think we could stop for lunch soon? I didn't eat breakfast this morning because my stomach was in knots just thinking about this trip. But now that I'm here and more relaxed, I'm starving."

"Sure, I'm famished too. Maybe it's all this fresh island air. Keep your eyes open for what looks like an inviting restaurant."

About ten minutes later, Kate pointed to a sign that read Sandy Cove Restaurant. They parked the car in a shady spot and entered. A hostess welcomed them, and led them to a table right beside windows over-looking the sparkling water.

"I think I've died and gone to heaven," said Dana in awe. "Look at that view with the mountains in the background and the water twinkling like diamonds where the sun's rays hit it. I've never seen such spectacular scenery."

"Just sitting here looking at it reminds me that we are so blessed to have a God who created such beauty," added Kate. She was interrupted by a chubby waitress who handed them menus in the shape of a fish.

They both selected one of the cheaper entrees on the menu, a fish burger and fries with coleslaw on the side. With a pleasant smile, the waitress assured them she would be right back.

"I don't want to spend a lot on food until we see if we are staying with my Grandmother. If we have to pay for accommodation, it'll take most of what I brought. I don't know if I can afford this trip, since my finances are still up in the air, but I think things will work out okay if I'm careful," explained Kate as she glanced around the busy restaurant.

"I was thinking the same thing. Since I'm considering a law degree, I've been extra careful with money. Nothing is definite yet. I'm still praying about it, but it sure will cost a lot."

The waitress returned with a delicious kaiser bun stuffed with a thick fish burger, golden French fries and a side of creamy coleslaw. There was minimal conversation except for groans of delight, as they packed away the scrumptious food.

"We've got to come back here before we go home," Dana exclaimed, wiping her mouth with her serviette. "That was the best fish burger I've ever had. I bet the fish came from around here, fresh from the ocean and into the pan. Another pound probably found its way to my hips. You're so blessed to have a slim, shapely figure. I bet nothing puts weight on you."

"I take after my Father. He could eat everything and never put on an ounce. It was a good thing because my Mother loved making butter tarts. She was known far and wide for her butter tarts. I'm afraid I haven't inherited her skill in making pastry. I've tried, but it never turns out flaky and light. Most times, it's so heavy that you could use it as a weapon."

Both girls shared a giggle. Kate was shocked. It was the first time she had mentioned her parents without crying and she had laughed. Feelings of sadness and guilt replaced the smiles and laughter.

"It's okay to laugh, Kate," Dana whispered. "I remember how guilty I felt when I started to really live again after losing my parents. Your Mom and Dad wouldn't want you to go through life in a state of sorrow and miss out on the fun experiences that might come your way."

"I know you're right. They wrote that in their letter, but it shocked me when I heard myself laughing. I think we'd better pay up and hit the road. How about I drive now and give you a chance to appreciate the scenery?"

"Thanks, Kate."

They had only driven for about fifteen minutes when a large, colourful sign at the side of the road indicated they were entering Qualicum Beach.

"According to the GPS, we're nearly at your Grandmother's. Do you want to pull over and pray before we get there? I know you must be feeling anxious about what she'll be like and how things will go." So Kate pulled over. They bowed their heads and Dana prayed God would direct them, protect them, and his will would be accomplished.

About five minutes later, the GPS directed them to make a left-hand turn off the highway into the laneway, which was hardly visible because of the mammoth evergreens on both sides. Fifteen feet ahead was a black iron gate blocking their path and a sign which read 'Private Property'. Next to the entrance was a green box with a button on it. Dana spotted it first and hopped out to press the button.

"This is the Grayson residence. How can I help you?" a male voice questioned.

"I'm Dana Moffet and I'm here with Kate Grayson. I believe Mrs. Grayson is expecting us."

"Yes, she is," responded the voice. "I'll open the gate. Please follow the laneway to the right. I'll meet you outside the house and show you where to park."

Dana hopped back in the car. The gate slowly opened, and they followed the very long driveway. Then, suddenly, the laneway widened into a large, cleared area and before them was a beautiful, stately Victorian home surrounded by a forest of evergreen trees.

Both girls were speechless.

"Wow, is all I can say," Dana exclaimed. Kate sat there in awe. She assumed her Grandparents were well off, but never in her wildest dreams did she imagine them living in a place like this.

A somewhat bald man, wearing blue jeans and a short-sleeved blue cotton shirt approached their car. His smile helped relax Kate, who was feeling more and more out of her depth.

"Welcome, ladies. I'm Bill and I work as a groundskeeper for your Grandmother. You can park over there. We park away from the trees because they have a habit of falling down, and I don't think you want your car underneath one if that happens. Please leave your vehicle unlocked for now and I'll bring in your luggage. Your Grandmother always has a nap after lunch. But I know she is eager to see you."

Thanking him and taking a deep breath, they approached the front door decorated on all sides with potted plants. A huge wreath made of artificial flowers graced the door itself. A lady with greying hair and wearing a dazzling floral apron answered their knock.

"Welcome. Come on in. I'm Sandy, Mrs. Grayson's housekeeper and cook. Looking directly at Kate, she said, "You are Kate, aren't you? I can see the resemblance to Mrs. Grayson when she was younger. You have the same gorgeous brown eyes and long, thick auburn hair.

And you must be Dana. We have all looked forward to your arrival. If you girls need to freshen up, the bathroom is over to the left or you can go into the great room and have a seat. Mrs. Grayson will be in shortly."

Thanking Sandy, they turned and entered the great

room, which was well-named. It was a huge room tastefully decorated in blue, green and gold tones, like nature had been replicated inside. The cathedral ceiling gave the room an open feel, and the massive windows going from floor to ceiling made you feel like you were sitting in the forest itself. They had cleared away enough of the trees to give a breathtaking view of the ocean with the snow-capped mountains in the distance.

"Oh my!" Dana exclaimed. "Have you ever seen anything like it? I could sit here all day and soak in the splendour of this scenery. I almost feel like I've entered the sanctuary of a church. How could you look at such beauty and not believe in God? The mountains and the tall evergreens are like arrows pointing up at Him."

"I was just thinking the same thing, and wondering how my Grandparents could look at this magnificent view and not be drawn to the Creator who made it?" Kate remarked as she continued to stare out the window, mesmerized by the scene before her.

Hearing the sound of footsteps behind them, the girls turned to see a slim, elderly lady wearing a pink silk dress with pearls. She was using a cane and walked slowly, but even at her age, she had a poise and bearing to be admired.

As she reached Kate, she stopped, smiled and looked longingly at Kate, as though she was saturating herself with every feature of her physical appearance.

"Girls, I want to thank you for coming. I know it was asking a lot after what Kate has been through the last few weeks, but there is so much that I need to discuss with you, Kate. I was so pleased when you said Dana could come as well. You are both so welcome in my home. Dana, please call me Lily. Kate, I'd be honoured to have you call me Gran, but Lily is fine if you are more comfortable with that. Now, tell me, how was your trip? Did everything go smoothly?"

"I was anxious," Kate explained. "It was my first experience with flying. But it sure helped to have Dana along. She had flown before, so she knew the ropes. Thanks to our map and the GPS on our smartphone, we found your home without a problem."

"We stopped at the Sandy Cove Restaurant, just outside Qualicum Beach, and had the best fish burger and chips," Dana said.

For several minutes, the discussion centred around the trip, the scenery and their lunch, giving them time to relax and get to know each other. The sound of the door opening drew their attention and Bill stood there balancing the luggage. "Lily, where would you like these to go?"

"The girls can follow you. I'll take the elevator and meet you upstairs."

The lovely, curved, oak staircase led to a second floor with spacious bedrooms off wide hallways. The door to the elevator opened and Lily carefully manoeuvred out and headed toward the first bedroom, asking the girls to follow. They found themselves in a room with immense windows, and wallpapered in off-white with pink rhodo blooms. An ensuite in the same colours was off the bedroom. The white dresser and end tables matched the white headboard, but the item that stood out above all others was the exquisite quilt on the bed.

Walking over to the bed, Kate turned to her Grandmother and asked, "Is this a handmade quilt?"

"Yes. About twenty years ago, when your Grandfather started spending more and more time at his office, I needed something creative to pour myself into to fill up the long hours when I was on my own. So I took some quilting lessons at a quilt store in Parksville and I found I enjoyed it. I required a place to spread out my fabric and make a mess, so we had a studio built onto the side of the house, and that's where I sewed and set up the quilting frame. There are seven bedrooms in this house and I've made a different quilt to go on each bed. Then, in the same fabric that I used on the quilt, I made a radiating star to go on the outside of the bedroom door. You didn't see it when you entered this room because the door was open, but on the way out, you'll see it."

"I love the fabric and colour combinations you used. Don't the patterns have different names?" Kate asked..

"Yes, they do. This one is called 'Wayward Rhodo'."

"It's been a goal of mine to learn to quilt one day, but with taking teaching-related courses, I haven't had the time. But I've done a lot of crafts and sewed many of my clothes," Kate said.

"Let me show you the other bedrooms, then you

can choose which ones you want," directed Lily as she slowly turned and walked down the hall.

Each room held new surprises, and each quilt was meticulously constructed and a work of art in its own way. Kate let Dana choose first and she decided on a room decorated in turquoise and lime green. Kate favoured the colour scheme in the first bedroom, and to her delight, it joined Dana's room with a sliding door.

"I'm going to need to lie down for a bit before dinner," Lily said in a somewhat weak voice. "It's usually around six o'clock. You girls unpack and feel free to wander through the house or the grounds and explore. My bedroom is the master bedroom, and it's on the main level next to the great room. I'll shut my door, so don't worry that you will disturb me."

Dana and Kate thanked her, and set about unpacking and commenting on the comfortable and classy rooms they could enjoy. When that task was completed, they were ready to tour the house. They descended the oak staircase to the great room. To the left of the great room was an arched doorway. They entered and found themselves in a dining room with an oval table and crystal chandeliers. Entering a door at the other side of the dining room led them to the kitchen. Sandy spotted them and motioned them in.

"We don't want to hinder your progress with dinner," Dana said.

"But if we can help in any way, we have willing hands," Kate added.

"Since Mr. Grayson died, we haven't had formal dinners. Our biggest meal is usually at lunch and then I leave something prepared for supper that Lily can just heat quickly, but I know she has hardly been eating anything. I made chicken soup and buns for our dinner. For dessert, we're having apple squares. So there was no fussing. At Lily's request, Bill and I will be joining you. You girls enjoy looking around."

Everything in the kitchen shone, from the quartz counters to the stainless steel appliances. There was an enormous amount of counter space and a family room off the back of the kitchen that also had floor-to-ceiling windows looking over the same vista as the great room. A gas fireplace was on low, and an oak table with pedestal legs was set for supper. Along another wall was a comfortable sofa and two reclining chairs. It was like a tiny house inside the bigger house. Sliding doors opened onto a very wide wrap-around porch. They were only about a hundred and fifty feet from the ocean. Dana was the first to notice an ocean liner passing by.

"That has to be a cruise ship!" Dana shrieked in excitement. "I've always wanted to go on a cruise. This is so exciting. Just sitting on this porch is like being part of an adventure. Have you ever sat on such comfortable chairs?"

Kate seemed perplexed and was watching movement over in the trees. "I think there's an animal behind those tall bushes.Watch behind the somewhat lopsided evergreen." The girls stayed perfectly still, watching.

"Oh look, aren't they the sweetest things?" asked Kate as a fawn and a doe emerged from behind the pine tree. I never understood how people could shoot these lovely creatures with their big, brown, innocent eyes.

"They are such gentle creatures, never attacking other animals," Dana agreed.

Just then, Dana's phone rang. It was her cousin Paul checking to see if she had arrived okay. After they chatted for a few minutes, Dana hung up.

"Paul's picking me up tomorrow morning on his way to the hospital in Nanaimo. He plans on having me back by lunch. That'll give you some private time with your Grandmother, so you can ask the questions you need answers to."

The dinner Sandy prepared was delicious, especially the apple squares. These are over the top scrumptious," Kate said as Sandy passed the plate of disappearing apple squares around the table."

"Thank you. I love trying new recipes."

Shortly after dinner, Kate's Grandmother announced it was her bedtime, but the girls were welcome to watch television, read or do whatever they usually did after supper.

"My cousin, Paul, is picking me up early in the morning, probably around seven," explained Dana.

"Bill, please make sure we leave the gate open for the entire morning," requested Grandmother. "And

Dana, bring your cousin back for lunch if that works with your schedule."

"Thank you, Lily. I'll certainly ask him."

After clearing the table and helping Sandy in the kitchen, Kate and Dana headed up the stairs to their bedrooms. It had been an eventful day and due to the time difference, both girls were ready to crawl under those amazing quilts.

chapter five

When Kate awoke the following day with the sun streaming in her window, she laid there thinking about how her visit was going much better than she had anticipated. They had received a warm welcome and lovely accommodation. She hoped her upcoming discussion with her Grandmother would not cause hurt feelings. There were things she had to understand about why her Grandparents had refused to have anything to do with her Father. The birds chirping outside and a particularly noisy woodpecker pecking on a tree beside the window had her rising, and thinking about how peaceful it was in Qualicum Beach. Kate glanced out the windows overlooking the woodland and the ocean at every opportunity she got. This was a place that grew on one.

On the nightstand, Kate saw her Bible. Sitting down on the bed, she took the time to read a section and pray that she would have a forgiving spirit as she talked with her Grandmother. She wanted to be a witness to God's love.

Kate dressed quickly in lilac-coloured pants with a matching floral top. Giving her beautiful auburn hair a hasty brush, she walked over to the sliding door between her room and Dana's. She knocked, but when she got no answer, she headed down the staircase to the kitchen. Sandy was busy making apple pancakes. Nicely browned bacon was sitting on a warming tray and orange juice had already been poured into dainty glasses on the table. Her Grandmother entered the kitchen just as she reached the doorway.

"You look lovely. Lilac is your colour," complimented Grandmother. "Did you sleep well? I hope the birds didn't wake you up. They have always been like an alarm clock for me."

"I don't think I woke up once all night. Has Dana got off okay?" Kate asked, looking at Sandy.

"Yes, she had breakfast and just as she finished and was getting up from the table to wait at the front door, there was a knock and her cousin was there. Dana asked him about returning for lunch and he said they would be back by twelve."

When breakfast was over, Grandmother suggested Kate come with her to her bedroom, the only room Kate hadn't seen so far. It was a cavernous room with two double beds, two bureaus, side tables and two reclining chairs. Like all the other rooms, the windows were immense, and a door led directly from the bedroom to the back porch. The room had a more masculine feel, with gorgeous matching quilts in rust, brown, beige and off-white. On one wall was a large, gold-framed photograph of a man. As soon as Lily saw Kate looking at it, she took her gently by the arm and they walked toward the photograph.

"I want to introduce you to your Grandfather," Lily said with tears in her eyes.

While Lily was making a valiant attempt to control her emotions, Kate looked at the Grandfather she had never known. He had a full head of grey hair that was immaculately cut, a rather long nose that reminded her of her Father and eyes that were a stunning blue, but did not have the twinkle that was in her Dad's eyes. A stern look on his face, almost a frown, made you feel like your presence wasn't welcome.

"I want to explain what happened between your Father and us. There'll always be the elephant in the room until you know what we did that ended up in your Father leaving and us never welcoming any contact. Let's sit in the recliners over there because this old lady doesn't have the stamina to stay standing."

"Your Grandfather and I met when I was nineteen and he was twenty-one. I went with a girlfriend to the movies one summer evening. During the intermission, I got up to go to the ladies' room and the bag of popcorn I had in one hand tipped, emptying the whole thing onto Al's head. He was sitting directly in front of me. I was horrified. He slowly turned, looked back at me, and said with a grin, 'I guess I had better thank the person who shared their popcorn with me'. After I apologized for covering him with popcorn and butter, we chatted for the whole intermission. Al asked me for my phone number as the movie was starting up again. I was more than willing to share it with this pleasant, good-looking young man with the most beautiful head of hair I had ever seen. We dated for three months and then he popped the question I longed to hear. On December twenty-ninth of that year, we were married and I can honestly say he was the man of my dreams." A few tears once again escaped from Lily's eyes.

"We didn't have much money but for three years before we met, Al had been working at the stock exchange doing mostly routine jobs of collecting mail, picking up information for the traders and things like that. He saved almost everything he earned. Al had been living at home and while he paid his parents board, he could still put most of his money in the bank. With what he saved, he bought us a cute little, and I do mean little, bungalow. While working at the stock exchange, he picked up a lot of knowledge about the stock market and how to invest. This was a whole new world for him because his father was a labourer and they never had more than just enough to live on.

"After we had been married for three years, I discovered I was pregnant. We were both thrilled and spent much of our time planning for the future. Al shared with me his dream to have his own company someday and be able to provide for his children and have them work with him as well. Shortly after Matt was born, Al decided it was time for him to put his knowledge to work by investing in the stock market. I was worried. What if we lost the precious little that we had been able to save? Al assured me that big money was to be made in the market. So he started researching stocks, reading portfolios on companies and talking to people who had traded in the stock market for years. Al invested all we had saved except the house.

"Everything he invested increased in value, and he more than doubled what he invested in a year. People on the stock exchange floor were now consulting with him when they were purchasing stocks for clients. After making sound investments for a few more years, Al decided it was time to branch out independently and open an investment office. Matt was around twelve when this decision was made, and from the moment it opened, Al reminded Matt that someday he would work with his Dad. Matt was still too young to fully understand the world of investing. He was more into baseball, soccer, and hockey. Unfortunately, Al didn't participate in or attend most of Matt's games because his sole focus had become the investment company. As his family, we weren't his priority. He spent long hours at work and even when he got home, he continued to do research in his office. I have to admit I was enjoying the fruits of his labour. We had a beautiful home in Vancouver, new cars every year, designer clothes and belonged to several social groups, which brought Al more clients. Later, Al bought this property and hired an architect to draw the plans for our house. In hindsight, I see how we gradually lost our real happiness in being a family and replaced it with pride in our social status and our bank account.

"When it was time for Matt to go to university, Al put a lot of pressure on him to get a business degree at the McMaster School of Business in Ontario. He had done his research and decided McMaster would give Matt the best preparation for coming in as a partner in the business. Matt knew how important this was to his Father. He had been hearing about this plan for years. Yet, something in me sensed he wasn't thrilled. Matt went off to McMaster in the fall and when he came home at Christmas, he told us about the friends he had made and he had joined a group on campus with a Christian focus. Al told him to stay clear of that group. They were probably a cult or religious zealots who carried things too far. Matt returned for Christmas, but I sensed that he and his Father were not on the same page.

"In mid-May, he returned home, having completed his first year with honours. We were both proud of him. But his plans for the future had changed. He told us he was now a Christian. He felt God wanted him to go to a Bible College in Three Hills, Alberta, to prepare him to serve the Lord and make this world a better place. Al totally lost it. I've never seen him so angry. Al's bubble, his plan for Matt, had burst apart with Matt's announcement. Al was about to discover something that we all do sooner or later–you can never totally control the decisions of another human being. All the bullying, lectures, insults, bribes, orders or physical threats are useless if someone is committed to an action, which in their eyes, is of utmost importance for their life to have meaning. Matt's goal was to help his fellow man, not make money working like a puppet on a string with his Father.

"Al accused Matt of being ungrateful and turning his back on the company that he had worked years to build for them to run collaboratively. Al's last words to him were, 'When you come to your senses, you knock on my door and tell me that you are prepared to be a partner in the business. Until then, we will have no contact with you in any way, and financially you are on your own. Make sure you have left by the time I get up in the morning.'

"At first, I went along with Al's idea of Tough Love, as they called it back then. We were sure that when he had to fend for himself, finance his education and live without the material luxuries he had access to in the past, he would be back. But as days turned into weeks and weeks turned into months and months turned into a year, I knew our plan for Matt would not be a reality. Matt tried to keep in contact by sending cards, letters and birthday gifts, but we never opened them. Al wrote 'Return To Sender' on any correspondence from Matt. He still believed that if we kept a strong, united front, Matt would return to take up a position in the business. Even the staff at our home and office were threatened with dismissal if they opened anything from Matt. His anger turned into bitterness and his employees felt the brunt of it. They weren't the only ones. We were seldom invited to social events because of his sullen and argumentative behaviour.

"Al was cordial to his clients and continued to make excellent investment decisions, so his work didn't appear to suffer. He poured all his energy into the company and worked longer hours. He often left for work before I got up and returned after I was in bed. I suggested he hire a bright young man or woman and mentor this person to be a partner. He refused. I know he never gave up hope that Matt would see the error of his ways and return to take over leadership of the business. After years of keeping the anger and bitterness bottled up inside of him, he had a heart attack. I hoped that would scare him into slowing down and making changes. Al closed the business, but he didn't sell the building. When I asked him why, he said the building was still a good investment. At eighty, and due to the heart attack, he didn't have the stamina he had before. He spent most days checking his stocks on the computer and reading."

"This had to be hard on you," sympathised Kate.

"He knew I was hurting over the no-contact rule of not seeing or hearing from Matt. This broke my heart, but honestly, I was so busy with social activities due to our position of wealth in the community that I didn't fully understand what I had been missing for a few years. Having lots of money can fill the hole in your heart for a while, but it doesn't last. I had a little money that my parents left me, which wasn't under the scrutiny of Al or his accountant. I decided a few years after Matt left that I needed to know how he was managing. I contacted a high school friend of Matt's and he told me he was living in Burlington. I got in touch with a private investigator, Garth Ellsworth, in Ontario and hired him to take pictures of Matt on or around his birthday without him being aware of it. I was not going against your Grandfather's wishes but it filled a void in my life. I rented a post office box in Qualicum Beach and Garth sent the pictures there. When the photos arrived, I was on cloud nine.

"They were of him at home doing yard work, at the mission in Hamilton that he started, and playing baseball with some other men. I contacted Garth after the first set arrived and asked him to do it every year. Al never knew about the photos until a few days before he passed away when I showed them to him. We both cried and for the first time in his life, I heard your Grandfather admit that he had made a mistake in trying to force his plan on Matt, and his anger had severed our relationship with him. I loved Al very much. But there were times when I had to rekindle that love by reminding myself of what he was like in our early days together before anger and bitterness consumed him."

Kate interrupted her Grandmother to ask, "How did he die?"

"Five weeks ago, he had another heart attack. An ambulance transported him to Nanaimo Hospital, where he was diagnosed with a severely damaged heart. The prognosis wasn't good. The doctor said he needed to remain in the hospital, where they could closely monitor his condition. I got him a private room and hired a nurse to be with him around the clock to keep him comfortable. Bill, our gardener, drove me to the hospital and accompanied me to the hospital room, where I visited with Al for an hour each day.

"One morning, the Chaplain came into our room. He is a young, energetic fellow with a friendly and compassionate manner. We just chatted about our lives and then he said a brief prayer and left. The next day, he popped in again and invited us to a short service in the meeting room down the hall. We agreed and two orderlies wheeled us both down in wheelchairs. The singing was joyful and uplifting. The Chaplain preached a short sermon on how God wants to forgive us and we, in turn, need to forgive others.

"The following day, Chaplain Paul stopped at Al's hospital room again and asked us if we had ever asked the Lord to forgive our sins. Thirty years ago, we would have been insulted if someone asked us that. We saw ourselves as the cream of the crop, the elite of society and money had put us there. Now, we were older and wiser with a whole raft of regrets. So we prayed with the Chaplain, asked the Lord to forgive our sins, and thanked him for being our Saviour. A new sense of peace and contentment filled our hearts.

"We told Chaplain Paul about how we had ruined our relationship with our son and hadn't seen him in forty-odd years. He suggested we try to locate him and mend the broken relationship. The last address given to me by Garth Ellsworth was in Burlington, Ontario. When I tried to reach him there, the number was now out of order. We figured he had moved."

"Yes, we all moved to St. Thomas when I got a teaching job there," Kate affirmed.

"Well, I contacted Garth again, and he said he would look into locating him. The same day that we became Christians in the real sense of the word, I showed the photographs that Garth had taken to Al. As I mentioned, we both got very emotional. Your Grandfather asked me not to contact Matt until after his funeral. He was so ashamed for letting his pride keep him from asking Matt's forgiveness for all those years. Al asked me to tell Matt he would be waiting for him in heaven. Your Grandfather died the next day due to heart failure and was buried in Qualicum Beach Cemetery. When I got home from the cemetery, Garth called and shared your Father's address with me. He couldn't find a telephone number, so he assumed it was unlisted. I sat down that night and wrote to your parents to inform them Al had passed away and invite them to come for a visit. Matt phoned me the day they received my letter and said they would be here on Friday. I was disappointed when he told me you couldn't come because you had arranged to take a writing course.

"Kate, I wish with all my heart that I hadn't asked them to come. I feel I'm to blame for their deaths. I've brought sorrow into your life and hurt the person I desperately want to love. God knows I never intended for any harm to come to them. I hope someday you can forgive me."

As Grandmother shared her story from her heart with Kate, the tears once again started to flow. Rising off the recliner, she walked a few steps over to her Grandmother, and bending down, put her arms around her. They stayed like that for several minutes as a bond of love replaced pride and unforgiveness.

Taking Lily's hands in her own, Kate spoke first. "I have always had a problem with anger. When I got word that my parents were dead, I blamed you. But after praying with Joanne, my friend in St. Thomas, I handed that anger over to the Lord and chose to forgive you. I know Dad prayed for you both. I was walking past his bedroom door when I was around ten and I heard him talking. I took a peek in and he was sitting at his desk, praying. I heard him mention several names and then he said, ' Lord, please have my parents accept you as their Saviour before they leave this earth.' What is so amazing, Gran, is that Dad and Grandfather are together again."

Hearing Sandy calling them for lunch, they got up and, hand in hand, walked into the kitchen where Dana, who had just got back, was introducing her cousin to Sandy. As Paul turned toward them to be introduced, Lily let out a shriek of joy. "Chaplain Paul, I had no idea that you were Dana's cousin!"

"And I didn't know we were coming to your home."

Lunch was further delayed while they hugged and chatted for a few minutes and Kate was finally introduced to Paul. He had not heard about Lily's son and daughter-in-law dying, so after they were seated around the table, he led them in a word of prayer.

"Father, we thank you for having a plan for each of our lives. Help us to daily seek your will and obey it to avoid taking detours that lead us out of your will. Be with Lily and Kate as they feel sorrow. But as your children, they have the hope of being with you and their loved ones when you call them home. Bless Sandy for preparing this delicious lunch and help us to use our strengths and abilities to help those in need around us. In your name, we ask this Lord. Amen."

Once they were eating, Dana shared about her trip to the hospital in Nanaimo to see where Paul worked. "We went to the Chapel first, and it is like a small sanctuary. Anyone who wants to pray or just find a peaceful place to reflect can go there. Paul drops in periodically throughout the day to see if anyone needs spiritual counsel. Then we went to the Palliative Care Ward and Paul went from bed to bed, chatting and praying with the patients and their families. I found that part very sad and I don't think I could do it day in and day out without getting depressed. Then we went to the meeting room ,where on Sunday afternoons, Paul plays his guitar for patients to sing and then preaches a brief sermon.

Kate interrupted at this point, "Paul, Lily told me just this morning that you led my Grandparents to the Lord. From the bottom of my heart, I thank you. My Father prayed for them, and I know he intended to try to discuss that with Lily when he arrived."

"Kate, the Lord speaks to the heart and draws people to himself. I'm just a tool in his hand."

Dana piped up again with more news. "On the plane, you mentioned you were supposed to be at a writing course this week. When we went for coffee in the cafeteria this morning, there was a community bulletin board and one ad caught my eye. There's a writers' and illustrators' conference on Tuesday and Wednesday in Chemainus. One of my hobbies is sketching and I have always thought I might like to do illustrations for children's books. Would you be interested in going?"

"That sounds wonderful. Do we have to register?"

"I copied down the phone number of the organizers. I'll call them when we finish eating."

A short time later, Paul said his goodbyes, promising to visit Lily again in the near future. Tired from an emotionally draining morning, Lily headed to her bedroom for a nap.

Kate and Dana had just finished helping Sandy tidy up after lunch when Kate's phone rang.

"Hello, Kate. It's Joanne. Hope I didn't get you at a bad time."

"It's good to hear from you. I planned on calling

you shortly to see if everything was okay in St. Thomas."

"Don and I are fine. We have continued to look for a rental but so far, nothing. So we might have to search elsewhere."

"There is no rush for you to leave. You can stay on for as long as you want, even when I get back."

"That's kind of you, but Don and I have never been ones to outstay our welcome. I've been busy sewing some new clothes. The ones that I wore on the mission field aren't suitable here. Don has been picking some delicious radishes and lettuce that your dear Father planted. I really called to tell you about something that is a concern for us. Stuart came around last evening after dinner and more or less demanded to know exactly where you were on Vancouver Island, and if we knew when you would be back. He didn't appear to be in a particularly good mood. We told him we were not at liberty to give out information, but he could phone you directly if he wanted the answers to his questions. He stomped away from the front door and roared out of the driveway in what looked like a very expensive sports car."

"As far as I'm concerned, Stuart is not part of my life and never will be again. I told him that. We are utterly wrong for each other. I appreciate you not giving him any information. He has no right to know about anything pertaining to my life. I'm shocked he showed up like that, and I don't know what he is up to. That concerns me."

"I'm very relieved to hear you say so. We prayed about the situation this morning and felt we should let you know Stuart was here. Just enjoy your holiday and don't let this put a cloud over it. How is your grandmother?"

"I have some wonderful news on that front. Both Grandparents became Christians the day before my Grandfather died, thanks to answered prayer and the Chaplain at the hospital. We had a long chat this morning and I feel like all those lost years have disappeared and there is a bond between us. She has made Dana and me so welcome here, and I feel like I still have someone in my family who cares about me."

"God's plan is unfolding, dear, and we will continue to pray for you. God Bless. Bye for now."

Dana, who had finished wiping down the quartz counters, turned to face Kate as she put her phone into her pocket.

"Did I hear Stuart's name mentioned?"

"Yes, Joanne told me he came around last night and wanted to know exactly where I was and I guess from his tone, he expected an answer, but they didn't tell him."

"He's got some nerve. What are you going to do?"

"I'll pray about it. I'm not out to hurt him but I want him out of my life.

They went for a walk down to the beach at Dana's suggestion. A couple of cottage-style chairs in a bright lime green with pink floral seat pads seemed to invite them to sit and enjoy the awe-inspiring view.

71

"Every time I look at the scene before us, I'm inspired to pick up my sketching pencils and create a masterpiece, but who could possibly come close to portraying the beauty that's everywhere on this Island? When people look at the magnificence of nature – those immense mountain ranges with green forests covering them and the water reflecting the blue sky, how could they not be moved to believe in God? His handiwork is a testimony to his existence. There is jaw-dropping beauty all around us. I always thought I would never want to leave St. Thomas. Most people feel a real connection to the place where they were raised. But this Island grows on you in a way that I can't put into words," Dana said as her gaze swept over the Strait of Georgia.

"You just said everything that I was thinking, although having not grown up in St. Thomas, I don't feel the connection you do."

"Could you leave your job and house in St. Thomas and move here?" Dana asked..

"I would miss teaching, unless of course, I could get a job here and I love the house we built in St. Thomas. I remember all the meetings we had with the builder planning it. My parents drove from Burlington each week to check on how things were progressing. On a few Saturdays, I made the drive, and couldn't believe how quickly a hole in the ground could be transformed into a house. But of course, the people in the house make it into a home, and now that Mom and Dad are gone, it feels empty. It has become just a house. St.

Thomas, is not what I was expecting. Since agriculture plays a role in the community, I expected a smaller city to be friendlier. So far that isn't what I have experienced. There are all kinds of churches around the city and I have visited at least half of them. The people would shake your hand and smile and comment on the weather, but there was no attempt to really get to know us. When we finally settled on one church to attend each Sunday, we joined groups to try and make real friends. I joined the Book Club, where everyone reads and discusses the same book. Mom attended the Ladies' Bible Study and Dad joined the Men's Coffee group. We even invited people in for dessert and tea. Yet, we still felt we were being kept at arm's length and were never invited back to anyone's home. Perhaps they already had a network of friends and didn't need us. But when I read scripture, I get a different picture of what the church should be like, and how brothers and sisters in Christ should genuinely care for each other."

"I'm so sorry to hear you experienced that, but I understand completely where you are coming from," sympathized Dana. "My church used to be warm and friendly. People would invite others to their houses every Sunday evening for dessert. So you got to know people below the superficial mask we wear most of the time. People who feel loved and not judged, open up about their struggles, conflicts, and needs. We prayed for each other and when a need came up, often someone had a suggestion on how to fill the need. But I noticed a few years ago how things had changed. It had been happening slowly. The church board discontinued the Sunday evening service. People stopped calling each other and invitations were rare. The practical needs of the congregation were often ignored. The pastor was no longer at the door on Sunday mornings to shake hands with the parishioners. New pastors came and went; most of them had never visited people in their homes or the hospital. Then numbers in the church started to drop. Right now, we get just enough donations to stay open."

"I wonder if it is only a problem in St. Thomas, or is it the same situation in most communities?" inquired Kate. "It would be interesting to visit a church on Vancouver Island and see what it is like, but we'd have to attend frequently to get a sense of what was going on."

"One thing we can do is pray for the churches," Dana suggested.

"I wonder if Gran is up yet. She mentioned that she'd like to show us her studio this afternoon."

"When we got home this morning, I noticed you called her 'Gran'. She noticed it too, I could tell," Dana commented. "She looked so pleased. Until then, I hadn't heard you call her anything."

"To be honest, I didn't feel it was appropriate to call her Lily," explained Kate as they walked back toward the house. "She had never been a real grandmother to me, so I didn't feel she deserved to be called 'Gran'. But after hearing her lengthy explanation of what had transpired for all those years, I felt that not calling her Gran

74

was judgmental and unforgiving on my part. She feels like a Grandmother to me now, and that is a precious gift from a loving God.

Strolling toward the house, they heard a loud tapping sound overhead. "Oh look," Kate said, pointing to the large Douglas Fir. "That has to be the biggest red-headed woodpecker that I've ever seen; much bigger than the ones in Ontario. I'm going to get his picture on my cellphone."

Upon entering the house from the porch, the girls saw Gran walking toward them.

"Are you ready to see my quilting studio?"

"You bet," Dana answered.

Gran pushed open a sliding door in what looked like the wall of the kitchen. They entered a room like many of the others in the house. Huge windows once again looked out over the forest behind them, yet a fair amount of natural light entered through several sky vents. Two modern sewing machines, one with a long arm, were positioned against a wall. An ironing board and a washer and dryer were along another wall. An oversized cutting table was in the middle of the room. On the third wall were organized shelves and cubby holes to hold fabric, thread, batting, and tools of the quilting trade, like rotary cutters and needles.

"This room is a sewer's dream," Kate said in awe. "I've been sewing since I was fifteen, but our sewing machine was in my parents' bedroom, and we placed a cardboard cutting mat on the bed to cut out our clothes' patterns."

"I'm afraid I'm all thumbs and no talent in the sewing department but this room is inspiring me to get creative," Dana admitted. "I didn't do well at school in the sewing classes. We had to make an apron and I sewed the pockets on upside down. I was okay in the cooking part of the program, so it pulled my mark up. At least I passed the course."

"I'd love to have you show me how to make the radiating star like you put on each bedroom door to match the quilt. They'd make unique gifts for showers or birthday presents," Kate said.

"I thought they were lovely too, but I suppose they are too difficult for me, being sewing challenged and all."

"They aren't complicated, and if we take it one step at a time, I'm sure you will have success. You don't even need to use a sewing machine," Lily added.

"Then let's get started. I'm in a creative mood," Dana said.

"Dana, could you kindly go to my bedroom door, and bring back that radiating star so we have an example in front of us?"

"No problem. I hope I lose some of the calories I put on at lunch."

As Dana left the room, Lily looked at Kate. "Kate, I'll be meeting with my lawyer and accountant on Tuesday morning here at the house. I know you and Dana are off on the writing and illustrating conference, but I want to ask you something. I hoped to make your

Father my Power of Attorney and Executor but that's not possible.

"Do you know what those roles involve?"

"Yes, my Mom did that for a friend who had cancer and died last year."

"Well, dear, I was hoping you'd consider doing that for me. I'll not pressure you into it. I'd like you to pray about this and if you think the Lord wants you to be involved, let me know before Tuesday and I'll inform my lawyer."

"I just love the colours you chose for this star," complimented Dana, who was reentering the sewing room holding Lily's radiating star in her hand.

"Picking out the colours and fabrics you want to use is the first step," Gran explained, ending her conversation with Kate.

"On the advice of my quilting teacher in Parksville, I only use one hundred percent cotton fabric. If you look carefully at my star, you'll see that I assembled it with alternating light and dark colours, so they set each other off. You need to pick out six fabrics that you like together. The tubs of fabric are over there on the shelves and I have the colour marked on the front of each tub. I love fabric and I'm afraid I go overboard when I enter a quilt shop. I'm like a kid in a candy store. The fabrics seem to speak to me and I have to bring them home. Feel at liberty to choose any you like. I haven't sat out on the porch since I went to the hospital. I think I'll get my Bible and enjoy the outdoors while you girls make your choices."

They spent the next hour moving fabrics around and deciding what combination worked best. The girls seemed to be in love with every fabric they pulled out, and before long, it looked like a bomb had gone off in the sewing room, with cloth covering the cutting table and various parts of the floor.

"Well," Dana said. "I'm satisfied my combination will work for me. I wish we could use seven different pieces instead of six because there is another one that I would like to include."

"I know what you mean. I always thought I was very decisive but there are so many beautiful fabrics that I keep changing my mind."

After cleaning up the floor and arranging their fabrics in order, they went to get Gran. She suggested they work together on the stars for an hour after supper tomorrow and Thursday. That way, they'd be finished to take home with them on Friday.

As Kate was preparing to climb into bed, she thought back over the last few days. She had worried so much about coming on this trip and how Gran would treat her. However, none of her worries had materialized and there had been unexpected blessings. She bowed her head, thanked God for those blessings, and asked his will regarding the roles that Gran wanted her to take on.

chapter six

Dana entered the kitchen to find breakfast had already started and apologized for not arriving on time. "I was just on the phone with Paul. He has offered to take us to lunch in Nanaimo, and then back to the hospital for his service in the Meeting Room. Lily, you have been to one of those services on a Sunday, haven't you?"

"Yes, dear, and I thoroughly enjoyed it. I'd love to go," Lily answered between sips of coffee.

"I'm in," Kate said.

"I told him he could pick us up at eleven if he didn't hear back from me. He said to dress normally, whatever that meant. Probably casual."

"I also got another call from the secretary who is covering for me at Mr. Howet's office while I'm here. Stuart came in on Friday and wanted a copy of your parents' will. Mr. Howet was at court, and the secretary told him she couldn't give that out without his permission. She said Stuart got quite nasty when she refused. What do you think he is up to, Kate?"

"I have no idea, but I'm uncomfortable knowing he is poking his nose into my business."

"Who is this Stuart fellow?" Gran asked.

"Someone I dated a few times back in St. Thomas before Mom and Dad died. He was handsome, immaculately dressed, charming as could be at first and he sold real estate. After their deaths, I saw a very different side to Stuart, and I didn't like what I saw. I told him it was over when he called at the airport. I can't figure out why he's still trying to find out information about my parents' will."

"Maybe when he doesn't get the information he wants, he'll move on. I'm so glad you were wise and ended it. Some girls hang on to the wrong guy so they won't go through life alone. I'm sure God has someone for you, and he will love you with his whole heart."

"I'll be delighted if he loves God first and me second," Kate said.

After enjoying a delicious breakfast of scrambled eggs and bacon prepared by Sandy, they all headed for their bedrooms to tidy up before Paul arrived at eleven o'clock. They no sooner got down to the front hall when the front gate buzzed. Gran pushed the release button in the hall and in a few minutes, they saw Paul's green Kia Soul pull up to the front door. Jumping out, he opened the doors for them, and told Lily to sit in the front where there was more leg room.

"Paul, what possessed you to buy a gr–ee–en car?" teased Dana as they proceeded up the lane and turned onto the Old Island Highway.

"Well, my inquisitive cousin, there were two reasons. One, green is my favourite colour and two, it is a very happy colour. People actually smile at me when they see my car. Anything that makes people smile or laugh is a bonus. I thought I'd take you on a brief detour around Nanoose Bay. The winding road will give you a view of some lovely houses and scenery."

"Is there any place on this Island where there isn't breathtaking scenery?" Dana asked.

Paul knew they were enjoying the excursion when he heard all the oohs and ahhs coming from the back seat. Headed back towards Nanaimo, they chatted away like old friends until they pulled into a parking lot outside of a place called the Beacon Bistro. It was built in the shape of a lighthouse and was right beside the water. Upon entering, they found a table that was so close to the water they felt like they could have put their hand out and touch it. Paul recommended his favourite dish, fresh-caught salmon, coated in a delicious light batter, and fried to perfection. That sounded yummy, so they all ordered it. After the first bite, the ladies gave rave reviews of the meal. These were the same ladies who, on the way to the restaurant, told Paul that they were so full from breakfast that they only wanted something light for lunch. By the time lunch was over, there wasn't a single French Fry left on anyone's plate. Even Gran had eaten everything, and seemed years younger than when the girls had arrived only a few days earlier.

"There are a lot of small planes taking off from the water," Kate remarked as she pointed to a spot down the beach.

"That's a flying charter service. Mostly business people charter a plane to fly them to the airport in Vancouver. Ferries are used frequently to get to the mainland, but take longer, so if money is no object or sooner is better than later, planes are popular. I've never been on a ferry because I don't like water, so I always take a plane. Mind you, I've only had to do so a couple of times."

Kate, looking confused, asked, "Why do you live on an Island if you don't like water?"

"Oh, I like looking at it, or fishing from shore or walking along the beach beside it. I just don't like being on it or in it."

"So when was the last time you had a bath?" Dana giggled. "It's pretty hard to take a bath without getting into the water."

Everyone, including Paul, laughed as he gave her a playful poke in the arm.

"Didn't you learn how to swim?" asked Kate.

"My parents forced me to learn to swim. A neighbour had a small swimming pool and he gave lessons. I don't think I've been swimming for at least eight years. The sensation of water surrounding me gives me the creeps."

Getting a serious look on his face, Paul told them he had something to show them that was a mystery to him. He extracted a small brown envelope out of his pocket.

"Since my parents died a year ago, I have been going through boxes out in the garage and getting rid of things like receipts, old letters and magazines. In one box with income tax papers, I found this envelope."

On the outside of the tattered and somewhat crinkled envelope was printing, smeared in places by what looked like drops of water.

"I didn't bring my reading glasses, Paul. Can you read it out loud?" Lily asked.

Taking a deep breath, Paul read, '*For My Child When It Is Time. Tell my child I love him or her with all of my heart. The locket is meant to be a reminder of my love. God Bless You, little one.*'

"What is stamped on the top left-hand corner?" Dana inquired.

"McMaster University," Paul answered.

"What's inside the envelope?" Kate asked.

"I used a pair of old scissors in the garage to open the envelope and there was this tarnished silver locket," Paul said as he carefully lifted out the locket. "When I pried it open, there were strands of blond hair and a picture of a beautiful young woman who I would guess is in her late teens. Dana, do you have any idea who this is a photo of? I wondered if your parents had any pictures of someone like her?"

"To my knowledge, I've never seen her before,"

Dana said, peering closely at the small picture. "Maybe, she is someone from your Mother's side of the family."

"It is a total mystery to me. I can't figure out why it was left unopened in a box in our garage."

Well, let's look for clues in what is said," Kate suggested. "I think she was probably a Christian from the words 'God Bless'. She seems to have written this before the child was born because she doesn't know if the baby will be a boy or a girl."

"I think you're right," Dana said excitedly. "I wonder what the first line means and the words 'when it is time'. Time for what?"

"I think we can assume the girl in the picture wrote that note," Lily said. " Paul, do you think it's possible that your Mother had a baby in her teens and gave it up for adoption? Maybe she intended to send this envelope along with the child but for some reason, she didn't do so."

"There is another possibility," Kate said. "You might have been adopted and your birth mother passed this envelope on to your parents, requesting that they give it to you. Maybe that is what 'when it is time' means. When they shared your adoption with you."

Looking bewildered, Paul shook his head. "They never indicated in any way that I wasn't their own."

"I have another possible explanation," Dana interjected. "Maybe your Mother had a friend who was putting a baby up for adoption, and she left this with your Mother for safekeeping but never returned to pick it up. Your Mother put it away safely and over time forgot about it."

"I'll give this whole thing a lot more thought, and maybe I'll find something else in the garage that'll give me more information. Dana's parents are gone and there is no other family to check with, so I won't solve this mystery any time soon. It looks like this place is getting really busy. We'd better free up our table."

Paul suggested he take a picture of them outside the restaurant, and then Gran offered to take a picture of Paul standing between Dana and Kate. He put his arm around them, and Kate couldn't help but feel a brief flutter. How she wished Stuart had been more like Paul. Paul was relaxed and had shown no signs of wanting to control people. He was taller than Stuart, and while Stuart was impeccably dressed, Paul seemed more casual.

With the constant conversation in the car, time seemed to fly, and they were at the hospital. Gran momentarily looked a little sad. The hospital reminded her of Al's passing. Paul offered to get a wheelchair for the long walk down the hall to the Meeting Room. Lily refused, saying she was feeling much stronger these days and the walk would do her good.

The meeting room was totally empty when they arrived, and Paul set about arranging chairs while Dana and Kate distributed song sheets and Gideon

Bibles. They were momentarily interrupted by a hospital volunteer who had a message for Paul.

"The pianist who usually volunteers is down with the flu, so I guess your guitar will have to provide the accompaniment today."

As she left, Kate said, "Paul, I can play the piano."

"Thanks. That would solve the problem. Dana, would you feel comfortable doing the Bible Reading?"

"I could but it might cost you another lunch at the Beacon Bistro before I go home."

Suddenly, the room started to fill with patients in wheelchairs, using a walker or in a couple of cases, pushed in on a gurney. Family members accompanied some of them and there was a sprinkling of nurses in case the patients needed their assistance.

After the group sang three of the old-time hymns and Dana read from the Bible, Paul began his sermon.

"My sermon today is titled 'When The Unexpected Happens'. Life is not predictable. We get up each morning expecting our life to unfold as we plan. Yet, on some days, the unexpected happens. We get fired from our job. We get into an accident. An appliance we rely on breaks down. A loved one gets sick or dies. These unexpected events never take God by surprise. What should our reaction to them be? We need to turn them over to God and seek his guidance. Simply pray, tell God how you feel, and ask for direction and peace. Then you must patiently wait and read his word. God speaks to us through the Bible. We are often under the mistaken idea that we are in control of our life, but we are actually in control of very little. So why not give everything that concerns you over to a God who loves you and understands your situation completely?"

At this point in the service, Kate thought about all the unexpected things that had happened to her in just a few weeks. Her Grandfather and her beloved parents had died, she broke up with Stuart, Dana had become a friend, she met her Gran and she was on Vancouver Island. Kate could feel God leading her.

Paul closed the service with prayer and then chatted with the people who had come. As the room cleared, he noticed a doctor talking with a patient on a gurney. As he approached, the doctor looked up and smiled.

"I wasn't aware that there was a service held down here. I arrived early for my shift and Mr. Buttle wanted to come to this service, but there was no one to bring him. Last week, he was able to use a wheelchair. Today, he just didn't have the strength. So I had the privilege of accompanying him. It looks like the room has emptied and I can get the gurney out the door now without causing any casualties. I enjoyed your sermon, Chaplain, and I hope to get back again soon."

Paul thanked the doctor for coming and spent a few minutes talking and praying with Mr. Buttle before they left.

"You preach a good sermon, Cuz," Dana said. "You keep it short and sweet."

"The first time I preached here, I prepared a long sermon like we were taught at Bible School. By the time I finished, all the patients were asleep and their family members had left. I got the message loud and clear."

Laughing, they all exited the hospital and headed back home, hoping that nothing else unexpected would happen in the near future.

chapter seven

During breakfast the following day, they discussed the envelope and the locket Paul had shown them. They agreed it was a mystery and must be a little unsettling for Paul.

"He has Monday off, so maybe he's hunting for more information," Dana suggested. "I'd be willing to help him. Maybe I'll call him."

"I'd be glad to help, too," Kate volunteered. "Give him a call now."

Dana left the room to make the call and returned, grinning. "Yep, he says he could use the help. I have the directions to his house. It's only about five kilometres from here."

After grabbing their purses and kissing Gran goodbye, they headed down the Island Highway.

"You know," Kate said. "I still don't have details

about how my parents died. I keep thinking about who would be the best person to ask."

"You could start with the medical examiner, Kate. I think he's in the basement at the hospital. Why don't you call and ask if you could speak with him?"

Pulling her phone from her purse, Kate had a short conversation. "His assistant said that he's busy doing autopsies this morning, but if I arrive around lunchtime, he would be available to see me. I have a picture of my parents in my wallet to help remind him of the people I need information on."

"It's about forty minutes to Nanaimo from here so if we leave Paul's place at eleven fifteen, we'll get there in lots of time."

"I appreciate your willingness to accompany me, but Paul needs your help. I could tell yesterday that this mystery perplexes him and must be solved. I wish I hadn't suggested that he might be adopted. He had such a doleful face for a few minutes after I mentioned it. Please stay and help him sort through the boxes. I'll pick you up on the way home from meeting with the coroner."

"This appointment could be tougher on you than you anticipate. I'm available if you change your mind and want some moral support."

They recognized the green Soul parked in the driveway and knew they had reached their destination. The garage door was wide open and they could see Paul already hard at work examining the contents of a box.

"Found anything to help solve the mystery?" Dana asked.

"No," Paul said. "To tell you the truth, I wish I hadn't discovered that envelope. But now that I have, I feel compelled to solve this mystery. These are the last three boxes. I appreciate the help because it's a very tedious process when you have to examine every piece of paper. I think my Mom filed everything that came into the house."

After getting the girls a chair and a table so they had room to examine the items, they all focused on the hunt for more information. They had only been sorting for an hour when Kate realized it was time to leave.

"Paul, I have a meeting in Nanaimo at twelve, so I must scoot. Hopefully, it won't take too long and I'll be back in time to help."

"Can I make you a sandwich before you go, Kate? I'm a terrible host. I didn't even offer you girls a coffee mid-morning. "

"I'm fine. I've done nothing but eat since I got to the Island."

"Yes, but at least it doesn't show on you," Dana commented. "I couldn't fit into a pair of jeans I tried to squeeze on this morning."

As Dana saw the rental car exiting the driveway, she leaned toward Paul.

"How are you doing since your parents' deaths? Wasn't it around this time last year?"

"Yes," responded Paul, not looking up from the box

he was sorting. "I miss them and I've put off doing this sorting because it brings back all kinds of memories."

"I experienced the same thing," shared Dana as she continued to watch Paul. "What was the official cause of death?"

All I know is that something happened on that boat and they both ended up in the ocean and drowned. The water patrol never found the boat. Another mystery, I guess. I know how Kate feels, losing both parents at once. It's a terrible shock."

"Is there anyone special in your life?"

"No, Dana. I'm not dating. I think the single life is best in my case."

"What made you decide that?"

"Before Dad died, he had to get a medical for work. The doctor told him he suspected Dad might have the beginning stages of Alzheimer's. It took several months to get an appointment with a specialist and they died in the boating accident before he got a definite diagnosis. When their bodies washed up on the beach, the regular medical examiner was on holiday, so they had a fill-in do it. He didn't check the brain, so I'll probably never know. Mom had noticed him forgetting things, and he had trouble focusing at times. She didn't feel it was safe for him to take the boat out and she told me the morning of the day they died that this would be their last trip. She intended to sell the boat. Dad was only in his mid-fifties. Apparently, Alzheimer's can run in families. My Grandfather also had it. I don't want to pass it to my children, make my wife a widow, or be burdened with caring for me. Besides, it's hard to find a Christian girl and I won't just settle for anyone. Mom and Dad were so much in love and truly enjoyed being together. If I ever do marry, I want a marriage like that."

"Have you had your eyes tested recently? Kate is a lovely girl both inside and outside. I've only known her for a few weeks, but I already feel like we're close friends. I've watched how she treats people and puts her Christian faith into practice."

"Kate will head back to St. Thomas, and you know as well as I do that long-distance relationships don't work. Anyway, she probably has a boyfriend back there."

"Well, she had one until just before we got on the plane. Stuart was probably the best-looking guy I've seen outside of the movies. No exaggeration. But his character left a lot to be desired and fortunately, Kate looks beyond the surface. The only problem is he keeps nosing around in her business and sends texts or phone calls trying to control her. I think it is starting to creep her out ."

Paul decided to focus on the sorting, and Dana followed his lead, hoping they would find something to explain the locket.

Kate could feel her level of anxiety rising the closer she got to Nanaimo. She was glad Paul had driven them to the hospital the other day. At least she knew how to get there without getting lost. She parked near the front entrance and locked the car. The doors to the hospital automatically opened, and she checked a floor layout on the wall to see where the morgue was located. Dana was correct. It was in the basement. She entered an empty elevator and descended. The morgue appeared to be straight ahead.

A small waiting area inside the doorway was empty. Noticing a bell on the counter, she rang it. In a few moments, a short, plump man with glasses and wearing a somewhat stained lab coat approached the counter where Kate was standing. After explaining that she needed to see the medical examiner and showing her driving licence as proof of her identity, he led her to an office with two seats. The gentleman extended his hand and introduced himself as Dr. Richards, the coroner.

"I'm here, Dr. Richards, to get closure over what happened to my parents. I live in St. Thomas, Ontario. I was in shock for the first couple of weeks, but now I just need to understand what transpired on the highway."

"Well, my dear, I can tell you what caused their death, but beyond that, I won't have all the answers you want. I can tell you who to contact for more information. Before I go on, I want to extend my sympathy for your loss."

"Thank you."

"I have your parents' file here. Although I see

94

numerous bodies weekly, I remember them well because we seldom get two from the same family. When we do, it's usually the result of an accident. The official cause of death for both of them was massive internal injuries resulting in excessive bleeding. Their injuries were extensive, the entire length of their bodies, and I suggested to the RCMP officer that his forensic team check out the car. Usually, if the airbags were properly deployed, there would be fewer injuries. However, people still die in accidents even when the airbags are working."

"Do you think they suffered?" Kate inquired as she held her breath and her eyes pleaded with the Doctor.

"No, they might have been conscious for a few minutes after the accident, but they were probably in shock and would not likely have been aware of any pain. I don't know what transpired on the highway, but I suggest you contact the RCMP office in Parksville. I have a card on my desk that gives you the address and phone number."

"I appreciate your kindness in seeing me. Oh, there was one more thing I needed to know. Who came in to identify the bodies?"

The Coroner opened his file and read, "A Mrs. Lillian Grayson, the mother and mother-in-law of your parents. Martha Weston, her nurse, drove her in. Mrs. Grayson was extremely distraught, and I feared for her health."

"But how could she when she hadn't seen my

Father in close to forty years and never met my Mother?"

"She brought recent photos with her that were taken by a Private Investigator in Ontario."

"I had totally forgotten about the pictures. Again, thank you, Dr. Richards."

As Kate climbed into her car, she decided her next stop would be the RCMP Office in Parksville. She hoped the officer who responded to the accident scene was on duty. Looking at the tide coming in as she drove along helped relax her. Kate thanked God that her parents hadn't suffered. That was one piece of information that eased her mind.

She found the RCMP station without difficulty, and a female officer at the front desk greeted her.

"I'm Kate Grayson. My parents were killed on the Old Island Highway almost three weeks ago. I don't know who the officer was that responded, but I would like to speak to him or her."

The officer immediately went to her computer and returned after a few minutes.

"Officer Hagen responded to that accident. He is about to go off duty. I'll see if I can catch him before he leaves."

Within minutes, Officer Hagen, a tall young man, walked briskly to the counter and introduced himself to Kate. He led her to his office, and they took their seats at a round table. A file was lying open between them.

"I'm sorry for your loss, Miss Grayson. It's a

terrible shock to hear that you have suddenly lost people dear to you."

"I think I'm getting over the initial shock, but I was very close to my parents, and I have to know what happened on that highway."

Looking over the file, he explained the events as he knew them.

"At around 1 pm on June 28th, a 911 call was received asking for assistance from both medical personnel and police at an accident scene on the Old Island Highway just north of Qualicum Beach. I was two cars behind your parents when the accident occurred, so I pulled my cruiser to the side of the road and ran to the scene. A young man, in tears, was leaning into the car trying to talk to your Father. I went to the passenger side to check on your Mother. I felt for a pulse, but there was none. I glanced over at your Father, and he briefly opened his eyes, looked at the young man and said, 'Forgiven' in a slow, weak voice."

Pulling the tissue from her pocket, Kate wiped her eyes and tried not to break into sobs. The officer waited for her to get composed before continuing.

"That was all your Father said. His eyes remained closed and when I reached the other side of the car to feel for a pulse, there was none. The ambulance arrived shortly after and they also checked for a pulse.

"I pulled your Father's wallet out of his pocket and his driver's licence indicated that he was from St. Thomas. A map in the car, which we presume had been on your Mother's lap before the crash, had a note taped

97

to it with a local phone number and an address. I phoned the number and Martha Weston answered. She put Mrs. Grayson on the line, who identified herself as your Father's Mother.

"I had to tell her about their death and overcome with grief, she passed the phone back to Martha Weston, and I gave her instructions about coming to the morgue to identify the bodies."

"What caused the accident?"

"According to the young man driving the other vehicle and two witnesses who agreed with his account, he was driving north when suddenly two deer, a fawn and a doe appeared in the middle of his lane. He swerved to avoid hitting them and went into the lane your parents were in, coming from the opposite direction. The road bends slightly at this point and he went right into the front of their car. One witness was a man outside trimming his grass, about one hundred feet from the accident.

"As I drove past this morning, I saw the same man erecting a small white cross at the spot where they were killed. The other witness was a Mother with her little daughter, who was blowing bubbles on the grass at the side of the road while they took a break from driving. We closed the roads to do measurements, take pictures and interview all concerned. When there is a death, I always take a breath test and observe physical behaviour for the presence of drugs. We also obtained a urine sample from the young man when we arrived here. Nothing showed up on the tests, so we are reasonably sure these things did not contribute to the accident."

"What will happen to the young man?"

"I don't know yet. He was released, but told to remain on the Island until the prosecution decides whether to charge him. Vancouver Island's economy is tied closely to tourist dollars, so when tourists like your parents die in a highway accident, it gets publicity and a call for making conditions safer and punishing the offender. Sometimes, it makes governing officials look better in the press when there is a conviction. Therefore, the crown counsel might be under pressure to charge him."

"The coroner told me the car was sent to a forensic team to examine. He felt there might have been a defect in the airbags," Kate said.

"I could tell at the scene something was wrong with the airbags because they didn't deploy to cushion your parents from the impact. The forensic team in their investigation, identified a poor installation job as the reason. The company, who produced the car, is sending their inspector out tomorrow to take a look. If they were partially responsible for your parents' deaths, they have a lot to lose."

"Officer Hagen, could I have the name and phone number of the young man who hit my parents?"

"I can give you his name. That's a matter of public record since it has been in the newspapers. But I can't release his phone number or address."

"Do you know if he has a lawyer and who it is?" Kate inquired.

Officer Hagen referred to his computer and shook his head.

"I know he had a lawyer. He called him when we asked him to come here and make a formal statement. His lawyer's name has not been recorded, so perhaps he didn't take the case. Also, according to the information on my computer, two pieces of luggage were found in the trunk of your parents' rental car when the forensic team had it towed here. The names on the tags were Matt and Becky Grayson. If you follow me, you can sign them out of the property room."

Kate had forgotten about her parents' luggage and was grateful the officer had brought it up. As she received possession of the baggage, she turned toward the officer.

"Thank you so much. I'm sure I've detained you from going home after your shift."

"Again, I'm sorry you had to come to our beautiful Island because of this tragedy."

Heading back toward Paul's house, Kate glanced at the time on her dash display. Getting answers to her questions had been more time-consuming than she anticipated. As she pulled into the concrete driveway, Kate saw Dana and Paul having a cold drink on the front porch. Kate reflected again on how different Paul was from Stuart. Her father would refer to Paul as a clean-cut, neatly-groomed young man. He was good-looking with a boyish kind of charm. His blond, neatly trimmed hair and solid, muscular build would probably qualify him for being described as a 'hunk'. So far, he seemed to be a genuinely kind and compassionate person, but time would tell, thought Kate, as she locked the car door and headed for the porch.

"I was getting really worried about you," Dana said, with a frown. "Where have you been all this time?"

"I couldn't get all the answers at the morgue, so I hurried over to the Oceanside RCMP office hoping to talk with the officer who was at the scene of the accident. He shared as much information as possible, even though he was off his shift. I think he has experienced grief because he was empathetic and didn't rush me. He even remembered that they had Mom and Dad's suitcases, so he turned them over to me."

"Hmm, was he young and good-looking?" Dana asked with a mischievous smile.

"He was young and all those officers look great in their uniforms."

"Would you like to share what you found out or just sit for a bit?" suggested Paul.

"Well, I guess the most reassuring piece of information was that my parents didn't suffer. Their deaths were quick. I now know where it occurred on the highway, and the young man who hit them swerved to avoid hitting two deer. There was a Mother with a little girl blowing bubbles on the side of the road, and I guess he couldn't steer that way, so he went into the other lane. A curve in the road blocks your view of what is coming, and his statement says that he didn't see my parents' car until it was too late. Officer Hagen told me his cruiser was just two cars behind my parents, and he ran over to the accident scene just seconds after it happened. When he got there, my Mother was not breathing, but my Father opened his eyes briefly and looked at the young man who had reached my parents' car ahead of him and said, 'Forgiven'. With his last breath, he showed love."

"Have they charged the guy who hit them?" Paul asked.

"Not yet. Officer Hagen said the prosecuting attorney was reviewing the case, but when tourists die on the Island, there is political pressure to convict because tourists are a big part of the economy. I'm determined to meet this young man. His name is Jerry Dunsmore. They wouldn't give me his address or phone number and didn't have his lawyer's name on file. I tried to locate his number on my phone before I left the station, but couldn't. Any ideas on how I can get in touch with him?"

"I play baseball with Christian guys every week during the summer. I have to leave shortly or I'll be late for our game tonight. One of them is a lawyer. I could ask him how we go about finding Jerry."

"That would be great, Paul. I feel in my heart that I have to speak with him."

They were standing up, ready to leave, when Kate realized she hadn't asked them if they had uncovered any more information during their hunt in the garage.

"Did you discover anything in the boxes that might throw light on the envelope?" Kate asked..

"Not a thing," Dana said. "But all that stuff is ready for the garbage, so at least the garage will look more presentable."

"I've checked through all the drawers in the house. There's nothing to explain the envelope and its contents. I'll continue to pray about it," Paul added.

The girls discussed the mystery on the drive down Old Island Highway. "I've been thinking about those theories we came up with at the restaurant that might explain the note and photo. Kate, I think your idea was the right one. Paul didn't look like either of his parents and didn't seem to have the same interests. I know that doesn't prove anything but I wish there was a way to know."

"I just got a brain wave," yelled Kate. "I've watched TV shows where a detective often finds a hair at the crime scene and takes it to a lab to get the suspect's DNA. Maybe Paul could take the hairs in the locket and see if they match his DNA. I don't know how they do it but maybe this would show if they're related."

"There are adoption registries too," Dana said. If she is Paul's mother, maybe she has gone on the registry looking for him.

"But we don't know her name," said Kate.

"No, but Paul could go on looking for her. Maybe he could give his birthday and his full name and she might see it and contact him."

"But Paul has the same last name as you, which

would not be the same as his birth mother's last name," Kate explained.

"This is not going to be easy, is it?" Dana asked with a perplexed look.

The tantalizing smell of Sloppy Joes greeted the girls as they entered Lily's house. Sandy had asked Kate while they were eating breakfast if there was anything she could make to remind Kate of home. The aroma from the kitchen brought back the memory of her Mom making their favourite supper. Kate felt tears welling up in her eyes. She still hurt from her loss, but the grief wasn't as overwhelming. She felt blessed to have the love and support of the people around her. Kate knew her heart was healing and Vancouver Island felt more like home.

"Dinner was ready half an hour ago," Gran said. "I was so worried that something had happened to you two. So I just called Paul's house to see if you were still there, but he didn't answer and I don't have his cell phone number."

"I'm sorry, Gran. I should've called. I got so caught up in my detective work this afternoon that I lost track of time."

Over dinner, they shared what had transpired as Kate visited various places to get information, and Dana assisted Paul in rummaging through boxes in the garage. Lily was pleased Kate had discovered details about the accident, as she had been too distraught the day it happened.

"Kate, if you can schedule a meeting with this Jerry fellow, I would like to go with you. And Dana, I'd very much like to help Paul find out who this woman in the locket is. If it hadn't been for Paul, neither my husband nor I would be Christians today. I can never repay him, but I want to do something."

After dinner, Lily suggested they go to her quilt studio and work on the radiating stars. The girls enthusiastically followed her, and carried out her directions for cutting the squares on the rubber mat with the rotating cutter. Next, she demonstrated how to fold the squares so they had triangles that were all the same size. They completed the first two rows of the radiating stars before they all found themselves yawning and heading for bed.

After tidying the sewing room, Kate caught up with Gran as she entered her bedroom.

"Gran, I have prayed about your request for me to be your Power of Attorney and Executor of your will. I'm honoured that you asked me and I'm willing to help."

Taking Kate's face in both hands, she kissed her on the cheek and said, "My Dear Girl, thank you so much. My attorney and accountant are coming tomorrow while you are at the Writing Conference. I'll give them the news and have them draw up the necessary papers. Sleep well, dear."

Kate looked out her bedroom window at the

amazing orange and red sunset and the moon shining down on the Strait of Georgia. Everything about this Island was capturing her heart, but she was supposed to leave in just a couple of days. She hadn't even explored her Grandmother's property, and it was full of nature trails that led to the cliff overlooking the water. Bowing her head in prayer, Kate thanked God for being with her today as she came to grips with the tragedy that had taken her parents' lives. She asked God to help Paul get a resolution to the mystery in his life, and to show her the plan he had for her life and help her to follow it.

chapter eight

The following day everyone was up early. Dana and Kate were too excited about the writing course to want much breakfast, and Lily was nervous about facing the lawyer and accountant on her own. Al had always dealt with financial matters, which annoyed Lily. He gave her the impression that women were incapable of dealing with such things. He should have prepared her for handling things on her own. She was convinced that he planned to outlive her, so why bother? Just another part of his plan that hadn't worked. Yet, she loved Al, despite his strange ways, and felt guilty for blaming him for her present situation.

Dana shared some news with Kate as the girls climbed into the rental car heading toward Nanaimo. "Last night, just as I turned the light off to climb into bed, my cell phone rang. It was the replacement secretary again. She had just gotten home but wanted to fill me in on what happened at lunchtime. Stuart arrived again and demanded to speak with Mr. Howet. She explained he hadn't returned from lunch. Just then, the office door opened and Mr. Howet walked in. Stuart demanded a copy of your parents' will. Mr. Howet, in no uncertain terms, told him he would not do so and that since he was not a client, he could leave his office. Stuart got an ugly look on his face. He accused Mr. Howet of turning you against him and dashing his dreams of owning a realty business. Stuart threatened to bad mouth him to his clients. Mr. Howet pointed to the door and told him to get out. He slammed the door with such force that two pictures fell off the wall."

"What happened to the charming guy I dated for a few months? Maybe he was like this all along, but I was swept off my feet by his good looks, great clothes and very expensive car. Was I that shallow a person? Dana, his behaviour scares me, and I feel so badly that Mr. Howet has to deal with this."

"I didn't mean to upset you, but I thought I should let you know. It's fortuitous that you came away on this trip and you aren't around St. Thomas to deal with his hissy-fits," Dana said.

"Changing the topic, I phoned Paul last night. I suggested he check out the adoption registries and maybe try to put his name on, even though we don't know his birth mother's name. I mentioned your idea of getting the DNA compared. He agreed to investigate both suggestions and let me know."

"I can tell this is bothering him. Yesterday, he

wasn't his usual joyful self. Just kind of quiet and withdrawn," Kate said.

When they entered the arena in Chemainus, they were welcomed by some volunteers and given a pamphlet listing the various seminars being offered for the next two days. They decided to attend the one titled, 'Write and Illustrate a Children's Story to Impress a Publisher' in the morning. Then, in the afternoon, they would go their separate ways. Kate wanted to attend the one on developing a plot. Dana was interested in learning about the different styles used for illustrations.

After an interesting and informative morning, they decided to use their one-hour lunch break to grab an ice cream cone and tour the town, renowned for its beautiful murals on the sides of buildings. Following the steps painted on the concrete sidewalks, they walked from one mural to another, getting a realistic picture of what this town was like in the past.

"I think my favourite mural is the one of some old fashioned-ladies standing in front of the telephone office. They were probably just as excited about the telephone coming to town as we are about our cell phones," Dana said, finishing her last bite of the chocolate ice cream waffle cone.

"I took a picture of the logging and sawmill mural. This is such a good idea to paint your town's history on buildings," Kate said, looking at her watch. "I think we'd better get back to the arena, or we'll be late for our afternoon sessions. I'm excited about writing a story that could become a children's book. I'll meet you back at the car when the afternoon seminars are over?"

Kate arrived at the car first, unlocked it, got comfortable and checked her text messages. Stuart had sent another text telling her he needed her to invest in the realty company soon, or he would lose the chance to lease a great building in downtown St. Thomas. Kate immediately sent back a text saying no money was available, and she didn't want him to continue to contact her about anything.

"Sorry I'm late," apologized Dana, as she slipped behind the wheel. "Are you mad at me?"

"No, why?" Kate snapped.

"You sound annoyed and your usual gorgeous face has a frown on it."

"I got another text message from Stuart telling me to hand over the money he wants. I'm fed up, Dana, but I don't know what else to do to get this to stop. It borders on harassment."

"When I return to St. Thomas, I'll ask Mr. Howet what he suggests. There has to be something that he can do to get Stuart to take a hike."

On the ride home, the girls shared what they had learned in their afternoon sessions and made plans to work on their radiating stars after dinner. Just before they sat down to enjoy a Macaroni and Cheese Casserole, Dana got a call from Paul. He had checked into the adoption registries, but you had to have a last name for the Mother and the birthplace would help too. Then he called a DNA facility in Nanaimo, and they said they couldn't get DNA from a strand of hair unless the root was attached. Paul checked the hair in the locket, but no roots were evident.

Dana returned to the kitchen to find everyone else sitting, ready to enjoy their food. After saying grace, she shared what Paul had told her.

"That is so disappointing," Lily said. "I wonder if it's the only DNA service available. Could one of you girls go on the internet after supper and see if there's another one?"

"We also want to work on our radiating stars tonight," Dana said. "I never succeeded in sewing anything, but my star looks great."

"The artist in you has an eye for colour," complimented Lily. "I'm eager to hear about the conference you attended today."

During the rest of the meal, Dana and Kate shared how they were inspired to write and draw. The window to a whole new world of creating stories that would entertain and educate children had been opened for them.

"Tomorrow, we meet and listen to published authors and illustrators share how they got started, how they work together and how they got published. Some self-publish and others hire an agent to try and get a publisher. I've already written a story about Cookie, a little Bichon I had until just a couple of years ago. I hope to get some ideas on how to improve it, or what editing steps I need to use to make it worthy of being published," Kate explained.

"Do you have a picture of Cookie with you?" Dana asked.

"I might have. I put some pictures in my suitcase to show Gran."

"Oh, that reminds me," Lily said. "I want to show you the pictures Garth took of your family on your Father's birthday every year. I must call Garth soon and tell him there will be no pictures this year," she added sadly.

After two hours of working steadily on the radiating stars, they sat back, tired but ecstatic over the outcome. Dana, who finished first, couldn't believe it was successfully completed, and looked good enough to put up in her apartment. Kate hadn't decided whether to mount it in her house or keep it as a gift. They both thanked Lily, who proved to be a patient and encouraging teacher. Gran suggested they go to the computer, and look up DNA facilities to see if there was more information on extracting DNA from strands of hair.

"I think I see something positive in this entry," Kate said. "It's a newspaper article about a Doctor in California who has developed a method of extracting DNA from old bones. As I read down further, it says he has used it to extract DNA from hair strands without roots. But since it is a costly process, it's not in common use. It can cost up to five thousand dollars."

"Dana, I need Paul's phone number," Lily said.

With his phone number in her hand, Lily walked over to the phone she kept beside her recliner. Paul answered on the second ring. "Paul, Kate just found some information on DNA testing done in California, and they don't need a root on the strand of hair."

"I read that when I was searching earlier, but it is extremely expensive, and I have other expenses like property taxes and house repairs to consider first."

"Paul, I appreciate everything you did for us in the hospital, and I have been looking for a way to show my appreciation. Please let me do this for you."

"Lily, my reward will be in heaven, and I know you appreciate what people have done for you."

"Al used to tell me I could be a very stubborn old lady, and once my mind was made up, arguing was a total waste of time. I want you to make arrangements with this lab in California to send the samples they need, and I'll make sure the money is available."

Just before hanging up, she said, "Paul, my husband spent his entire life accumulating wealth. I want to spend the rest of my life investing in people. That's the Lord's plan for me, and like my son, no one will stop me from following His plan."

The girls, who had been listening to this one-sided conversation, realized what a transformation there is in a life when it is given to the Lord.

"Oh, Gran," Kate cried. "Dad would be so pleased to hear you say that."

Kate walked with Gran to her bedroom and hugged her. Just then, her phone rang. Frowning at the interruption, Kate took it out of her pocket.

"It's another call from Stuart."

"Dear, why does he keep calling you when you have broken up?" Lily asked.

"He thinks I inherited a lot of money and the house. I told him that according to the will, I couldn't do anything with the house or touch the savings in my parents' bank accounts for a year. There is only a couple of thousand dollars in the bank. My education was expensive. Believe me, Stuart needs at least a hundred thousand dollars for what he has planned. I've made it clear several times that he is getting nothing. I regret ever dating him. I'm not a very good judge of character."

"What is Stuart's last name?" Lily inquired.

"Coghill," answered Kate. "Good night, Gran. Thanks again for teaching us how to make radiating stars."

"You're welcome, Kate. I'll see you in the morning, Lord willing."

Closing the bedroom door, Gram looked at the clock and walked over to the telephone to call Garth Ellsworth. She told him about her son's death. But then Lily asked him to investigate Stuart Coghill. She explained about Kate's relationship with him, and how he was hounding Kate to sell the house and hand over her parents' savings. Lily told Garth all she knew about Stuart, and suggested he start by visiting him at his realty office.

Garth agreed to ask specifically for Stuart on the pretext of finding out house prices and availability in St. Thomas. Apparently, he knew a detective on the St. Thomas Police Force, and he would see if he had any information. Garth promised to get back to Lily as soon as he had anything to share.

chapter nine

"I wonder which authors and illustrators will be at the conference today," Dana said as she spread raspberry jam on her toast.

"I'm thinking back over all the books I read to the children in my class. I hope I have enough imagination or creativity to write something that could get published. I'll compile a list of the books they display today, and try to get the librarian at our school to purchase them when she goes book shopping. She hasn't been selecting as many books since less money is allocated every year to the library. More money is being designated for technology."

The drive to Chemainus went smoothly. The girls couldn't help but remark on the incredible scenery along the way. A couple of deer were at the side of the road, and Dana slowed down on the chance that they might dart out. Boats were already sailing on the water that sparkled like diamonds as the sunlight hit it. As always, magnificent mountains like giants rose from the water and reflected into it. Breathtaking landscapes were everywhere.

Authors from the Island and mainland took the platform to share how they and the illustrators collaborated to create a book worthy of publication. Both Dana and Kate jotted down any hints and suggestions that might come in helpful as they embarked on this adventure in creative writing. Before they realized it, the morning session was over.

"Why is it that time goes by so fast on this Island?" Dana asked as they walked down the main street of Chemainus, enjoying a Danish Pastry from the local bakery. "Our visit is just about over, and I don't feel like I've started to see everything. Kate, you have the entire summer off. Why don't you stay on with your Grandmother?"

"I was thinking about that last night as I laid in bed, listening to the waves lapping against the shore. I feel so much more relaxed here. But I don't like to think of you taking the return trip by yourself."

"The trip is only four hours on the plane. My car is at the airport. I'm fine going back by myself."

A ringing cell phone interrupted their conversation. After a minute or so of listening to the person on the other end, Kate shared her news with Dana.

"Paul offered to drive me to an appointment at a lawyer's office to meet the young man who drove the truck that hit my parents. It's for ten tomorrow. He has sent the materials needed to test for the DNA to the university in California, and he should have the results in a few days."

"I hope it's not too upsetting for you to meet this young man. I wanted an opportunity to do some illustrations, so while you're gone, I'll get started. If you give me a summary of your story on Cookie, I'll attempt to draw some pictures to illustrate it. Would it be okay if I worked in the quilt studio? That room is inspiring."

"It's a great place to work so you won't be interrupted," Kate said as they entered the arena for the afternoon sessions."

"Dana, I have to make a phone call. Can you save me a seat? I'll be right in,"

Grabbing her phone out of her purse, Kate hit the numbers for Mr. Howet's office. Unexpectedly, he answered.

"Mr. Howet, it's Kate Grayson speaking."

"Hello, Kate. I was just thinking about you."

"Oh, is there something else related to my parents' deaths?" Kate inquired with a puzzled look.

"No, something related to Stuart Coghill," Mr. Howet answered in a serious voice.

"Dana told me that he came into the office demanding a copy of the will," Kate said.

"Yes, he did, and I told him to leave – empty-handed. Has he pestered you for a copy, Kate?"

"No, but there have been numerous texts and phone calls wanting any money I have available for an office he plans to open. Every text is increasingly demanding, and I've repeatedly told him I don't want any more contact. This has gone beyond the point of being annoying to scary. I haven't told Dana or my Grandmother about all the texts, but I can't continue with this constant harassment. I wondered if there was anything you could recommend."

"We can go directly to getting him charged with harassment. Or I can write a letter warning him we will proceed with getting him charged with harassment if he doesn't stop contacting you immediately."

"I'd rather have you write the letter first and give him every opportunity to stop this behaviour. If he doesn't, I'll proceed with the harassment charge."

"I'll have my secretary type the letter immediately and deliver it to his realty office when she goes out at lunch. He'll have it early this afternoon. Kate, don't erase any of the text messages, and if you can tape any future phone calls, please do so. They are evidence if he continues making himself a nuisance. I'll keep a copy of the letter on file here."

"Thank you, Mr. Howet. I pray the letter will stop him and my life can return to normal."

"You are very welcome, Kate. Another client of mine was here this morning, and apparently, Stuart has used a scheme to make money off his clients that is unethical. He is bad news on many fronts."

After hanging up with Mr. Howet, Kate quietly entered the seminar, which had already started.

The afternoon sessions strengthened Kate and

Dana's determination to write and illustrate a book together. The conference's presenters assured them they weren't in this alone. They would get lots of support from the publishing company. Both girls had been praying about this and felt the Lord was leading. Once again, his plan was unfolding.

"Just think," Kate said as they entered Lily's house. "Three weeks ago, we met for the first time. I feel like we are kindred spirits, both on a journey, going in the same direction. I never had a sister, Dana, but I feel like I have one now."

"I feel the same way."

Over supper, Kate shared Paul's call from earlier and told Lily that if she still wanted to meet with the young man who had caused the accident, she was welcome. Lily, most definitely, wanted to meet him.

Taking their coffee out to the porch, they all found comfortable chairs and sat back, watching a variety of boats – some small like kayaks and others almost as big as cruise ships. Lily shared about the trip to Hawaii that she and Al had made on a cruise ship many years ago. By the light in her eyes, as she recalled the trip, Kate could tell that there had been some happy times for them, not just regrets.

Kate couldn't help but think that marriage, for some people, seemed to be a complicated mess of highs and lows, rough patches and smooth slides. In contrast, for others, like her parents, it was a consistent and exhilarating path where love and respect dominated every aspect of the journey. That was what she wanted, or nothing at all.

She had to wonder why Paul's face came to mind. She appreciated him offering to come with them tomorrow. Kate didn't know what she would do if the young man she was meeting tomorrow had a flippant attitude about what he'd done to her parents. She would have to pray about her reaction. Kate believed that she had forgiven him but had she really? God knew her heart, and she could go to Him with anything.

The buzzer on the front gate announced Paul's arrival at nine-fifteen. Lily and Kate didn't expect him that early so they grabbed their purses and said goodbye to Sandy working in the kitchen. Dana had already started sketching in the quilt studio.

"Lily, this is a nice surprise. I wasn't expecting you today. Are you sure you're up to the emotional strain of meeting this young man?" Paul inquired with a concerned look.

"Since Dana and Kate arrived, I've been eating much better, sleeping like a baby, and I feel ten years younger. So, to answer your question, I need to meet this young man. I'm putting my trust in God now, so don't you worry about me."

A huge grin spread across Paul's face as he gave Lily a quick hug and helped get her seated in the front with him.

"Kate, could you please open a window back there, so we get some air circulating? We don't get much humid weather, but today will be an exception."

"No results from the test yet?" Kate asked.

"No, I think it's too soon."

The lawyer's office was located in the downtown area of Nanaimo in a relatively new building overlooking the water. Paul parked underground, and they took the elevator up to the ninth floor. An elaborate foyer led into a waiting room with winged chairs covered in a velvet-like material. It was obvious that a very skilled interior decorator had been hired to create a posh first impression. A friendly secretary, who reminded Kate of Dana, asked them to have a seat. Kate was surprised when she felt something cold and wet on her elbow. A golden retriever with beautiful brown eyes was looking at her.

"Well, hello there," Kate said laughing. Paul and Lily turned in their seats to see the dog licking Kate's elbow.

"She introduces herself to everyone," the secretary said. "You wouldn't believe how many people come here focusing on their problems, and just worried sick about some issue. But after they spend a few minutes patting Chester, they go into Mr. Baskin's office totally relaxed. That dog has been the best thing to happen to this office in a long time. It's in my job description to take him out on a regular schedule for walks. I've lost pounds since he arrived six months ago."

"He's such a well-mannered dog and his coat just shines," Lily observe.

"He's always been friendly but his manners needed a little work, so Mr. Baskin took him for obedience training. His coat was a total mess when he arrived, but regular visits to the groomer and getting brushed daily at home have resulted in his gorgeous coat. Chester was found in the park tied to a garbage pail and from there, he went to a rescue."

"I volunteer with a rescue group in St. Thomas. Many animals, no fault of their own, are tossed away. I've been thinking about getting another dog. But my situation at home has changed, and I don't think it's fair to have a dog if he has to be kept inside all day while I'm at work," Kate said.

Hearing an office door open, they all looked up. Mr. Baskin, a tall, middle-aged man with greying hair and a moustache to match, walked toward them and after introducing himself, they entered his office.

Inside the office was a circle of chairs to accommodate six people. Two men sitting on the chairs rose as they entered, and waited until the ladies sat down before sitting themselves. Mr. Baskin introduced Mike Harding, a lawyer and Paul's friend, and Jerry Dunsmore, the young man they were there to meet.

"Ladies, on behalf of all three of us, I'd like to extend our sympathy at the passing of Matt and Becky Grayson. We've all lost someone, at some point in our lives, and we know the sorrow and emptiness that leaves. Jerry is here voluntarily. When I phoned him to relate your wish to meet, I told him that he was not obliged to do so. However, without any hesitation, he accepted the invitation. I'm here as his legal council and Mike Harding is here as a witness," Mr. Baskin explained.

"We're here to get closure and the details of what happened to the people we love. I've visited the morgue and the RCMP offices in Parksville. We would like to hear what happened from Mr. Dunsmore himself," Kate said, looking over at Lily, who nodded in agreement.

"I'll relate the events from that day to the best of my memory," Jerry said as he cleared his throat. " I left the Value Pet Store in Parksville to deliver bags of dog food to Comox. I was headed north on the Old Island Highway. Just north of Qualicum Beach, I suddenly saw a doe in the middle of my lane and a fawn just starting into the lane. The maple trees on the right-hand side of the road cast large shadows over the road, and I was literally on top of them before I realized they were there. I had only seconds to respond. To my right were a mother and a little girl playing in front of their parked car. To my left, there was a turn in the road. I couldn't see if anything was coming, but to avoid hitting the deer, I took a chance and moved across the yellow line, and into the lane for oncoming traffic. I braked as I saw a car in my path, but we slammed head-on almost immediately. I jumped out of the truck and ran over to their car. I was yelling, 'Are you alright?' It was obvious that they were not okay. The lady was unconscious. Just as the gentleman opened his eyes, an RCMP officer arrived. He tried to get a pulse from the lady, but I could tell from her face that she was gone. The gentleman didn't move except to try to open his eyes. He looked directly at me and said, 'Forgiven'. At that point, I lost it and collapsed on the ground crying. The ambulance arrived shortly, and their bodies were removed from the car. Both were declared dead at the scene. The car was towed away and the truck was impounded. The RCMP officer asked me to drive with him back to the station to make an official statement. He gave me a breath test at the scene, and when we got to the station, they asked for a urine sample which I provided. I can assure you that I wasn't speeding, and I don't drink or take drugs. The officer asked to see my cell phone. I guess he checked to see if I'd been on it at the time of the accident. I wasn't.

"Before I gave my statement, I called Mr. Baskin and he came over to the station. He asked me if the airbags had deployed, and I suddenly recalled that they hadn't. When he shared that with the officer, he told Mr. Baskin he'd noticed the same thing, and the forensic people would be looking into it.

"I want to tell you how much I regret making the decision to go into the other lane. If I'd known there was a car coming, I wouldn't have done so, even if it meant hitting the deer. I love animals, and there's something inside me that wouldn't let me kill them if I could avoid it. I'm so very sorry for putting you through this and killing the people I know you loved. I wish it had been me that died that day, and if there was any way to go back in time, the outcome would be different. I don't deserve your forgiveness so I'm not going to ask for it. I take full responsibility for what happened. I don't know what my punishment will be, but be assured, I'll not fight it."

While Jerry was sharing the details of what happened, both Lily and Kate reached into their pocket for a tissue. Paul had taken Kate's hand in his and Kate had reached out to take Lily's hand. When Kate glanced over at Jerry she could tell that he was trying not to break down.

"Mr. Baskin, could we meet with you for a few minutes privately?" Kate asked with a sniffle.

"Mike and Jerry, I have some coffee in my office. I'll meet you there shortly," instructed Mr. Baskin.

"Everything Jerry just said lined up with what I was told at the morgue and the RCMP office," Kate said.

"Can you tell me anything about Jerry's background?" Kate asked.

"Yes, I can share what I know.He was placed into the foster system when he was three years old. His parents were arrested numerous times for selling drugs, so social services removed him from the home. His first foster home was loving but after three years, the Mom became ill and had terminal cancer. They had three children of their own and the Father felt overwhelmed. So Jerry was moved to a second foster home. It started out okay, but marital problems around finances resulted in a divorce, and they had two children of their own, so Jerry ended up in a third foster home at the age of ten. This couple was in their late fifties, and they had raised their own children who were gone. They wanted to provide a home for a child in need. They supervised his school work, took him to his soccer games, and he accompanied them to Sunday School and church every week. There are very few parents in the foster system like them.

"Jerry graduated from high school in June with honours and a scholarship. He decided to work for the summer to save money for university. He was accepted at the University of Guelph in Ontario for the fall semester. Jerry wants to be a veterinarian. He has always loved animals, and since he was fourteen, he has volunteered at a rescue in Nanaimo on Saturdays. I first met him there when I visited the rescue looking for a dog. He introduced me to Chester. I assume you met him in the waiting room. He's my official greeter," Mr. Baskin said, smiling."

"What do you think the judicial system will do to Jerry?" Lily asked.

"You might disagree with me, but I don't think Jerry should be charged. If I'd been driving that truck, I'd have made the same decision that he did. When we've only a split second to decide, there's no time to second-guess what you're doing. This is a fine young man, who has his whole life ahead of him to help animals, and it would be a crime to see him go to jail and waste his time and abilities. I do fear they might charge him due to political pressure. This Island makes a lot of revenue from tourists. When tourists get killed, it's not good publicity and politicians like to give the impression the problem is solved by putting someone in jail. I've been trying to talk him into letting me fight against this, but so far, he wants to be punished. I'll do anything I can for him pro bono. His foster parents have retired and just moved to Florida, so he doesn't have anyone here in his corner."

Kate looked over at Gran and could read from the kind smile on her face that they were in agreement.

"Mr. Baskin, we don't want Jerry charged. He had a tough decision to make and I'd have made the same one. Could you arrange for us to speak with the Crown Counsel in the hope of them not proceeding with charges?" Kate asked.

"Yes, I'll most certainly try to arrange a meeting. Would tomorrow be convenient ?"

"Yes, and can my Grandmother and I speak briefly to Jerry?"

"Yes, but I need a witness there. Mike will join you."

"That's fine," Kate agreed.

Jerry was sitting in a chair, looking drained, as they entered the other office. Kate walked over and said, "We forgive you, Jerry."

With shaking shoulders and tears streaming down his face, he said, "I don't deserve it."

"Jerry, God has forgiven us for our mistakes and he wants us to forgive you. He has a plan for your life, and I think you have a good idea of what that is. Trust him to work things out, and when they do don't look back and let regrets pull you down. Go ahead knowing you are forgiven," Lily said as she wiped a few more tears from her eyes.

They hugged Jerry goodbye, and Lily and Kate went back out arm in arm. When they were seated in the car, Paul led them in prayer for Jerry and their meeting tomorrow with the Crown Counsel. Now they could leave the details with God, and go home for another one of Sandy's delicious dinners.

chapter ten

After supper, Dana and Paul went out on the porch to enjoy the view over the water. Lily poked Kate on the arm and asked if they could talk for a few minutes. Then, she led Kate to the recliners in her bedroom, where they wouldn't be interrupted.

"Kate, I know you are supposed to leave the Island and return to St. Thomas after the meeting with the Crown Counsel tomorrow. I just want to tell you how much your visit has meant to me. I realize now what I've missed all these years, not having you and your Mom and Dad in my life. But that's the past, and Lord willing, I'll have some time left to enjoy loving you. When I met with my lawyer the other day, he made you my executor and power of attorney. I invited my accountant because I wanted to know more about my finances. As I mentioned before, your Grandfather managed everything, and as it turns out he did an even better job than I imagined. There are millions of dollars in our accounts. I've been reading my Bible a lot lately, and I used the concordance at the back to look up verses pertaining to money. I was surprised to read so many verses with instructions on how we are to handle it. I want at least half of what's in the account to be used for worthwhile charities, some that are already doing a great job of helping people or starting some new projects where there's a need.

"I require someone to oversee this who has a heart for people and will make sure the money is used as I intend it to be used. I'd very much like you and Paul to oversee this. Neither one of you will make decisions without praying about it, and this money is owed to the Lord. Your Grandfather gave very little to charities. We need to do much better in the future. I know this is a big decision for you, so what I want to suggest is that you stay for another month and see how this idea of mine works out. If it doesn't, then you still have your job and house in St. Thomas."

"Gran, you know I love you and this Island. It feels like home after only a week. But when it comes to handing out huge sums of money, I've no experience with that at all. What if I make a mistake? I'd feel awful. I think you need someone more experienced than me. Also, I was a terrible judge of Stuart's character, so I'll likely get conned again."

"I have no worries whatsoever about you. Your experience with Stuart will actually profit you in the future. You'll no longer take anyone at face value. The

Lord will guide you and Paul as to which charities or people need the money. I haven't spoken to Paul yet about this, but I've prayed about it. I wanted to speak to you first in case you didn't want to work with Paul. You will both receive a salary, and my accountant will work under you. I read a Bible verse last night and it said, 'I can do all things through Christ who strengthens me.'

"Gran, I'll try my best for a month," Kate conceded, smiling. "I think I'll enjoy working with Paul, but time will tell. I want to encourage you to follow God's plan for your life by helping others with the money he has given you. And look at you, quoting Bible verses at me."

Gran leaned over and gave Kate another hug. Lily felt God had another plan for Kate that she wasn't aware of, and Gran was already playing a part in that too.

As Kate and Lily headed for the back porch to join Dana and Paul, the phone rang and it was for Lily.

"Hello, Mrs. Grayson, Garth Ellsworth here. I have some information for you about Stuart Coghill. Is now a good time?"

"Yes, Garth. What have you uncovered? I'm going to put you on speakerphone so Kate can hear."

"I got in touch with my detective friend, and he was able to use his resources to obtain some information that I wouldn't be able to get. Stuart has been the subject of a couple of harassment complaints. One was made while he was at college in his final year. The female student claimed that Stuart sweet-talked her into doing many of his assignments for him, and when she stopped, he got verbally abusive and controlling. She ended the relationship but he wouldn't take no for an answer.

"The second complaint was from a secretary at the real estate office where he was employed in Oakville. He kept pestering her to invest in his business after he found out her aunt had recently died and left her an inheritance.

"Both women felt that he was capable of physical abuse, but it hadn't happened so far. Apparently, he had his act of being charming down to a science, and it was so convincing that before anyone realized it, Stuart had wormed his way into their lives and was controlling them. He has a habit of picking out the people most likely to cooperate. People who go to church are usually gentle, kind and not confrontational. They believe in turning the other cheek and forgiveness. But some, like Kate's parents, were also wise and could see through the deception. From what you've told me, they took steps before the trip to protect their daughter."

"Oh my, others have been hurt just like my Granddaughter."

"After I finished speaking with my Detective friend, I drove to the realty office in St. Thomas where Stuart works. I asked specifically for Stuart. He came to the outer office immediately and was extremely welcoming and personable. Then he led me to his private office, where I asked him to tell me about bungalow prices in St. Thomas. He printed off several pictures of homes for sale. Just as he finished, a colleague came into the office. I assume he ran the business, and he told Stuart they needed to speak as soon as he was free.

"However, it appeared as though Stuart was in no hurry for this meeting as he offered to take me to see the homes. I told him I'd look over the printouts, and if I was interested, I'd contact him. I left his office and hid behind an artificial palm tree where I could keep him in sight. I observed Stuart walk across the hall and into the boss's office. It was obvious from the tone and volume of what the boss was saying that he was extremely upset. From the conversation, I gather that last night he asked Stuart to put two for-sale signs up on some properties. Since the signs were already in the boss's car, he told Stuart to take his car and return it to the parking lot by seven forty-five so he could leave for a showing. When the boss went out at seven forty-five, he noticed small brown specks all over one side of the car. On his way to the showing, he went through a car wash but the specks wouldn't come off. In a very loud voice, he demanded to know where Stuart had been with his car.

"Stuart informed him, with a snarl, that he had put up the signs and returned directly to the office. He implied that someone had done the damage after he returned it. Stuart's face was beet red and he started flexing his fists. I could tell his anger was escalating and there was no sign of the charming version of Stuart

I had seen earlier. The boss said he wasn't buying his story, and Stuart was going to pay for a paint job. Stuart raised his fist, seemed to think better of it, turned and stormed out of the office. Seconds later, he roared out of the parking lot in his sports car. Lily, I'm not a psychologist, but I have seen narcissistic behaviour before and Stuart fits the profile. Your Granddaughter should be careful and have no further contact with him."

"Thank you, Garth, for uncovering all this information and for observing Stuart in action. I know Kate has no interest in pursuing a relationship with him. As a matter of fact, she just shared with me today that her lawyer has dropped off a letter to Stuart warning that a charge of harassment will be next unless he stops contacting her."

"Lily, men like Stuart seldom take warnings. But I hope I'm wrong. Contact me if there's anything else I can do. You know, Lily, in the thirty years that I've worked for you, I've never met you. I hope to change that someday."

"Vancouver Island is a beautiful place for a holiday, and you would be welcome to stay here, Garth."

"That's a very tempting offer. Take care, Lily,"

Just as Gran hung up from talking with Garth, Kate's cell phone rang.

"Miss Grayson, the meeting for you with Crown Counsel is scheduled for eleven tomorrow morning at the courthouse in Nanaimo," Mr. Baskin said.

"Thank you for arranging it. Goodnight."

The doors to the back porch opened and Paul and Dana entered the house. Paul thanked Lily for dinner and wished the girls a safe trip back to St. Thomas. As Paul left for home, Gran headed for her bedroom.

"Dana, I just had a long talk with Gran and she has requested I stay on for at least another month to help her set in motion some plans she has made. Are you sure you feel okay about flying back by yourself?"

"No problem. This is a great opportunity to build a relationship with your Gran."

"Also, I have to attend that meeting with the Crown Counsel tomorrow."

"I hope you can convince them not to prosecute," Dana said.

Pointing to the sofa, Kate said, "Sit down for a minute. Unknown to me, Gran contacted a private investigator she had used previously and had him investigate Stuart. While you and Paul were on the porch, he called to share what he found out. It's late and we are both exhausted so I'll give you the short version. There've been reports of Stuart harassing other women and just yesterday, he had a heated confrontation with his boss over returning his car with tiny brown specks of something all over one side. I'm glad Mr. Howet had the letter delivered to him yesterday as a warning to stay away from me."

"Thank the Lord that you aren't back in St. Thomas. Staying here with Lily is definitely the safest choice."

As they headed to their bedrooms, both girls

mulled over the information about Stuart and prayed he would no longer be a problem in Kate's life.

As the sun was just starting to rise, Kate was awakened by Dana shaking her gently. "What's wrong?" Kate asked as she tried to focus.

"I just got a call from a very distraught Mrs. Howet. When Mr. Howet didn't get home by nine-thirty, and he didn't respond to phone calls or texts, she called the police and asked them to go over and check his office. The door to his office was unlocked. When they entered, they saw his cell phone on the floor, papers scattered all over his usually tidy desk, and files in one filing cabinet were in a jumble, sticking out at weird angles. They started a search of the building and found him at the bottom of the stairwell – dead. They wondered if he might have had a heart attack, and fallen down the stairs, but with the state of the office, they are unsure. The coroner will have to do an autopsy. I'll drive right from the airport to his office since they need me to check to see if anything is missing."

"Oh, Dana," Kate whimpered. "How awful! Mr. Howet was so kind and caring when my parents died."

"He was a generous and respectful boss too. I don't know what this means as far as my job goes. I know he was considering retirement and had quietly shared his intentions with lawyer friends hoping they might hear of a young lawyer starting out who'd like to take over his clients. He told me he'd try to turn over his practice to someone who'd keep me on as a legal secretary. I phoned the airport and I can get on an earlier flight this morning."

"You can return the car we rented when you arrive at the airport. Gran said she has one in the garage I can use. I'll give you my share for the charges."

"Are you kidding! Lily has fed me all week and I've lived in the lap of luxury. You owe me nothing. But I sure will miss you."

After a brief hug, Dana returned to her room to continue packing while Kate knelt beside her bed, asking the Lord to get Dana home safely, comfort Mrs. Howet during this tragedy that had changed her life, and be with Kate and Gran as they speak with the Crown Counsel.

An hour later, as Dana was packed and ready to leave, Lily took her aside.

"Dana, my dear, I want you to feel welcome here any time and stay for as long as you want. To think that I didn't know you a week ago and now you feel like another Granddaughter to me. I'm praying for you and asking the Lord to send you back here."

"Every time I look at my radiating star, I'll remember to pray for you too. Thank you for your hospitality and Lord willing, I'll be back."

After more tears and hugs, Lily and Kate stood in the doorway waving goodbye as Dana drove up the lane towards the highway and back to the airport.

Kate and Gran grabbed their purses and headed for the garage. At Gran's instructions, Kate typed a code in the box outside the garage and the door went up. Inside was a luxury Mercedes with a glossy silver finish.

"This looks like a very classy car. Are you sure you want me to drive it?"

"Yes, dear," Gran said with a smile. "I haven't driven this car in a year. Bill drove it when he took me to the hospital to see Al each day, but other than that it has not been used. I guess I can still drive, but I find it so much more relaxing to let someone else do it. Also, my eyes don't seem to be good for night driving."

The drive to Nanaimo went smoothly. Kate couldn't believe how well the car handled and that it had all the latest safety features. The leather seats had a lot of back support and Kate felt she could drive forever without feeling the fatigue that was usual in most automobiles.

They located the offices for the crown counsel without difficulty, and as soon as they entered the doors a secretary took them to the office of Mrs. Stevens. They were just nicely seated when a short, thin woman in a well-tailored navy suit entered and introductions were made.

"Mr. Baskin set up this meeting and told me you wanted to discuss the accident on the Old Island Highway where two tourists lost their lives," Mrs. Stevens said as she sat in a tall wooden chair behind her desk.

"My parents and Mrs. Grayson's son were killed in

the accident just over two weeks ago. I live in Ontario and I came here to find out what happened, and hopefully get closure. In speaking with the police officer on the scene, the coroner, and Mr. Baskin's client, I think we have a very good understanding of what transpired. Are you familiar with what happened, Mrs. Stevens?"

"Yes, I've reviewed the case several times. I'm assuming you favour the young man being charged since this resulted in a personal loss."

"No, absolutely not," Lily said, leaning forward. "We believe that nothing positive would result from charging Jerry, and I think if any of us had the same choice to make that day, we'd have swerved to avoid the deer. He's a fine young man who regrets what happened. He's willing to face the consequences and throw away a scholarship to the University of Guelph to become a vet because he feels so much guilt. Jerry in our opinion, has been punished enough, and we're asking that no charges be laid."

"Well, this is a first," said a stunned Mrs. Stevens. "When I'm asked to speak with people who have lost loved ones due to an accident, they usually want me to throw the book at the driver. I agree that this young man seems to have a positive future in front of him and circumstances seemed to make his decision that day impossible. However, there is some pressure from above me to take this case through the courts."

"Ms. Stevens," Lily said with a determined look in

her eyes, "If this goes to court, we'll hire the best criminal attorney we can find. My husband, who died a month ago, was very influential on this Island and invested in several newspapers. I still have contacts there and in the internet services. I'll pull out all the stops if this young man has to go through a court trial to make a few politicians look like they have fixed a problem where no problem exists. That is not a threat. It's a promise."

Rising from her chair as a signal that the meeting was over, Mrs. Stevens said, "I'll bring a committee together to review the case again and let you ladies know the result. Please leave your phone number with my secretary."

Once they were back in the car, Lily turned to Kate and said, "Did I come on too strong?"

"You were great!" shouted Kate. "Gran, I didn't think you had it in you. I was speechless. Women in power positions sometimes respond better to a direct approach. I'm sure that right now, she's on the phone checking out your connections. You've probably rattled a few cages. Just the threat that you could use the press to make the crown counsel and the politicians look like fools will make them think twice about going ahead. But we have even a better resource. The Lord knows what was in Jerry's heart and what plans he has for him. We need to continue to pray that His will be done."

"Yes," agreed Lily. "His way is the best way even if things don't work out the way we want. But sometimes

141

he gives us the privilege of helping that plan along," Lily said, with a mischievous smile.

After taking a scenic drive back to Qualicum Beach, they had a quiet lunch on the porch. Sandy had made raspberry cream cheese muffins while they were gone. " Sandy," Kate shouted from the porch. "I've never tasted such yummy muffins. I usually don't eat more than one muffin, but I couldn't stop at one today."

"I'm so glad you enjoyed them. It's a new recipe I clipped out of the newspaper. You, ladies are my guinea pigs."

Lily's outing seemed to have tired her so she excused herself to take a nap. Kate missed Dana. Grabbing her phone, she dialled Dana's number, figuring she was probably back in St. Thomas. After several rings, Dana picked up.

"Are you back in St. Thomas?"

"Yes, I arrived about thirty minutes ago and the office is a mess. The police had it taped off as a crime scene since the coroner told them that the autopsy showed he had been in an altercation with someone. Mr. Howet had a lot of bruising on his face and chest. They wanted me to inspect the files and see if anything was taken. The files under C and G were jumbled. Mr. Howet had a safety box hidden under his desk where he kept anything that he was currently working on. I checked it because the police wanted to know if there was a case he was involved in that would have resulted in someone wanting to silence him. When I checked the safety box, I found a copy of the letter that was delivered to Stuart and another interesting document about Stuart's scheme. A client of Mr. Howet's came to him three days ago because he put an offer in on a house through Stuart. Even though the offer was for more than the other offer, Stuart did not show the seller his offer."

"That doesn't make sense," Kate responded. "Why wouldn't he show the seller the higher offer?"

"That is where it gets interesting," continued Dana. "The couple with the lower bid told Stuart that they desperately wanted the house. So Stuart suggested that if they made it worth his while, he would only approach the seller with the one offer, their offer. From what I read here from Mr. Howet's notes, Stuart got an extra fifteen thousand for himself. The seller never knew there was a higher offer until the next day when the couple with the higher offer went for a walk.They saw the seller outside his house and told him they were disappointed that he hadn't accepted their offer.

The seller asked them how much their offer was for. The seller realized he wasn't even told about the offer. He called Stuart and told him he was going to his lawyer. Mr. Howet had almost completed the paperwork to fax to the Realty Board of Ontario. I showed all of this to the police."

"Do you think Stuart had something to do with Mr. Howet's death?" Kate asked.

"Well, so far, I haven't found anything else Mr. Howet was working on that would have anyone upset enough to hurt him. He handled mostly real estate transactions and wills, nothing related to criminal cases. Also, when I checked the files, the Grayson file was missing. Kate, I don't want to alarm you but Stuart was the only one I know who would be interested in that file. It contained a copy of your parents' will and the letter they wrote to you. If I hadn't known you personally, I would probably not have noticed that it was missing. Please be careful until the detectives on the case interview Stuart."

"Stuart doesn't know where I'm staying. I'm okay," reassured Kate.

"Tell Lily I'm putting up my radiating star as soon as I get home. That was the best holiday I've ever had. Need to run. There's a really good-looking police officer standing in my doorway, obviously wanting some more information. Bye, Kate."

As Kate hung up, she had to smile at Dana's obvious interest in the male population. She hoped Dana didn't get hurt as she had. Getting involved was a huge risk, a risk that she hadn't anticipated. A risk that she was determined not to take again.

Opening the door to the porch, Kate saw Bill with his wheel barrel and a shovel headed towards the house. She waved and Bill turned toward the porch.

"Looks like you've been working hard."

"There's still a lot to be cleaned up out here after the winter we had. More snow than usual and a few trees came down. This property seems bigger every year, but that is probably because I'm getting older. As much as I get a lot of pleasure out of gardening, my arthritis doesn't seem to appreciate it."

"Maybe you need some help out here, Bill, especially for summer clean-up. I'll suggest that to Gran."

"Kate, I don't want to worry you, but I saw what I think are cougar tracks near the service road that enters the west side of the property. They are well away from the house, probably four or five acres over but it pays to be careful, especially at night."

"Cougars. I had no idea there were cougars on Vancouver Island."

"Yes, there are hundreds of them. They are nocturnal, so people don't see them often and it's been quite a while since any attacked or killed a human. There's a steady supply of deer on the Island for them to eat."

"Thanks for the heads up," Kate said.

As Bill continued his trek towards the large outdoor shed, Kate heard the sliding doors open and Gran approaching. She was positively beaming .

"I just received a call from Mrs. Stevens. They've decided not to press any charges against Jerry. She said she was personally very pleased that we were not interested in vengeance, and she felt justice was better served to let all concerned make the most of the rest of their lives. I thanked her and I told her we prayed that the right decision would be made. She has already contacted Mr. Baskin and he will let Jerry know."

"Oh, Gran, our prayers were answered. But then, God always answers our prayers. Sometimes they are not answered the way we want but his ways are the best. "

Sitting on the porch overlooking the ferns and wildflowers, Kate and Gran discussed Bill and perhaps it was time to hire someone to help him. The conversation turned to coyotes and Gran explained that there had only been eight cougar-related deaths on the Island in a hundred years and in all her time living in this home, she had never seen one. She did, however, caution Kate to be aware of her surroundings, but not to live in fear.

"Is there anything that you are afraid of, Kate?"

"The only thing I'm fearful of is falling into another relationship. I've decided I'll be polite to guys but keep them at arm's length. The single life looks a lot more appealing to me. I don't have to wonder if I can trust someone."

"If God's will is for you to remain single then that is the right choice. But if he brings someone special into your life, your soulmate, and you push him away, then that is something you will regret for the rest of your life. I think right now you are hurting from how Stuart treated you. Not all men are like him. Your heart will heal, and then you will be ready to love again, and you will choose more wisely."

The buzzer sounded on the back porch, alerting them to a vehicle that sought entry through the gate. Kate entered the house and spoke through the microphone. It was Paul wanting to speak briefly with Kate and Lily. Kate pressed the button to open the gate. By the time she got to the door, Paul had parked and he and Jerry climbed out of the car.

"Where is Mrs. Grayson?" Jerry asked.

"We're out on the porch. Follow me," answered Kate leading the way.

Lily had risen from her chair to see what was going on. Jerry ran over to her and embraced her in a gentle bear hug.

"I want to thank you, ladies, for speaking to the Crown Counsel on my behalf after the sorrow I've brought to your lives."

"We had only a small part in God's plan. We don't believe He wants you in jail," Lily said.

"I want to tell you about my faith," Jerry said, as they all found a seat on the porch around the glass table.

"My last foster family, the Durkins, are Christians. They took me to Church every Sunday, and they lived a life of love and forgiveness. When I went to live with them, I heard for the first time that God loved me, and he sent Jesus to die on the cross to take the punishment for my sins. I asked Him to forgive me and be my Saviour when I was thirteen years old. The church had a huge young people's group and we were involved in all kinds of wholesome activities, which kept all of us out of trouble. When this accident occurred, I had to wonder where God was. If He loved me, why did something so horrible have to happen? After about a week or so of trying to come to grips with the whole mess, I turned all of my concerns over to Him. He knew I didn't mean to hurt anyone and if the law said I deserved jail time as punishment, then I'd accept that as his will. I wondered if he needed me in jail for a reason. Then Mr. Baskin called me a couple of hours ago and told me what you had done. That blew me away. Mr. Baskin called Mr. Harding, who in turn called Paul. He phoned to congratulate me, and I told him I wished I had your number to thank you. Paul said he could pick me up if I wanted to come and thank you in person."

"So what are your plans now, Jerry? You have college in the fall, don't you?" Kate asked.

"Maybe. You see, the pet store I was working for fired me when the accident occurred. The truck I was driving had been damaged and they thought I'd be charged, so they hired someone else. I didn't feel I would be considered for another job until I found out if I was going to jail. I've been searching for a job on the Internet but there aren't many. I'm sure God will provide a job if he wants me in college."

"Kate and I heard of a job opening this afternoon. Our groundskeeper, Bill, told Kate that due to his arthritis, he's finding the work here a challenge. We decided we'd hire someone to assist him. It would be from 8 am-4 pm, Monday to Friday. It pays minimum wage but there's a bonus at the end of the summer if, in our opinion, you tried your best. Don't feel obligated to take this job if it doesn't appeal to you. Not everyone likes landscaping and gardening."

"Next to animals, I love gardening. The Durkins

had an oversized lot, not as large as this property, but they expected me to help by cutting the grass, weeding the lawn, trimming the bushes and doing other garden-related jobs. I'd like to accept the job offer. When do I start?"

"Tomorrow. I'll let Bill know he has an assistant and you will report to him each day. Bill is your boss and he needs to be respected as such. I'm assuming you have a car. When you arrive tomorrow, go down the service road on the west side of the property. It'll take you to a storage barn, and you can park there and walk along the trail back to here. I'll tell Bill you will meet him here at eight o'clock. Lunch will be whenever Sandy is ready to serve it, and you are welcome to join us. That bell over there is what we ring to get everyone back to the house."

"I've got an older car that sometimes leaks a bit of oil so I'm glad to park it at the storage barn. Thank you again for your kindness towards me, and I'll certainly try not to disappoint you."

Lily turned to Paul and asked him to join her inside for a few minutes. "Paul, I'd like to offer you a job as well. I know that you have a full-time assignment at the hospital. This would only be a few hours each week. I had a meeting a few days ago with my accountant, and in the past, we did not give hardly anything to charities. I want you and Kate to help me decide what charities to support, or if new charities need to be started. There are several million dollars that need to be dispersed between them. You and Kate would receive a salary for your work. I need people I trust to help me with this."

"I'm honoured you asked me, Lily, but I'll have to decline."

"Do you feel it's too much on top of your job as Chaplain?"

"No, that's not the problem. I can't work with Kate."

"Why ever not? Have you two had words over something?"

"No, Lily, just the opposite. I'm very much attracted to your Granddaughter. She serves the Lord and is a lovely girl, inside and out, as Dana so eloquently put it. But when my parents died last year in a boating accident, they did an autopsy on them but didn't check my Father's brain. He was showing signs of memory loss and was only in his early fifties. Alzheimer's can run in families. I don't want to leave my wife a widow at an early age or pass it on to children. I always dreamed of finding a girl like Kate and starting a family, but I have to do the responsible thing. It would be torture to come here every week and work with Kate knowing that all we could have is a friendship."

"I respect your reasons for refusing, but I think you are wrong. You need to pray about this, Paul. None of us have any guarantees when we enter a relationship, but to pass up a soulmate that God has brought into your life, even for a few years, seems such a waste."

"I'll pray about it, but I don't expect anything will

change my mind," Paul said with a downcast expression.

"That's all I ask," Lily responded, as she hugged Paul.

Shortly after the men said their goodbyes, Sandy served supper. Kate said the blessing and thanked God for their answered prayer and his faithfulness in all situations. After dinner, Lily pulled out the pictures Garth Ellsworth had sent over the years. Lily and Kate sat on the large sofa with an equally large coffee table in front of them and had lots of room to arrange the photos. At times, they both got teary-eyed as they looked back at happy times in Matt's life with his family. Kate knew she had been blessed to have such loving parents. From the pictures, it was easy to see that her parents loved each other, and that love had flowed over to her. Lily, once again acknowledged how much she had missed in life. This made her more determined than ever to enjoy the time she had left with her granddaughter.

chapter eleven

The wind picked up overnight and blew the humidity off the Island. The air blowing in the window was definitely cooler as Kate woke up under the cozy quilt on her bed. She pulled on her slippers and walked to the window that looked down on the ferns and wildflowers growing under the rugged evergreens. Kate could see Jerry and Bill heading toward the back of the property and hoped they would find each other a blessing. After dressing in casual cotton pants and a long-sleeved t-shirt, she headed down to the smell of bacon frying. Lily was already up and thoroughly enjoying a baked apple pancake swimming in maple syrup and topped with slices of fried bacon.

"Kate, did you think to call your friends in St. Thomas who are house-sitting for you to let them know you're staying on for a month?"

"With all that's been happening around here, I totally forgot."

"You realize if someone my age used that excuse, they would say I was having a senior moment," teased Lily.

"I'll phone them as soon as I finish breakfast," Kate said as she bit into her apple pancake. "I sure hope they can stay on. I don't like to think of the house standing empty."

"Have you heard any more from Stuart?"

"No, nothing since Mr. Howet had his secretary deliver the letter to him. But when I called Dana yesterday, she said she found paperwork in Mr. Howet's secret safe that told about some scheme Stuart had cooked up to get people to pay him several thousand dollars more to make sure their offer went forward. Mr. Howet was going to fax the paperwork to the Realty Board of Ontario. Stuart would probably have lost his licence. The coroner concluded from bruising on Mr. Howet's body that he was in an altercation with someone. I keep wondering if Stuart is responsible for his death."

"I certainly hope not. But Garth felt his anger was escalating. I'm sure the police will thoroughly investigate," Lily said.

Rising from the table, Kate collected the dirty dishes and filled the dishwasher. After thanking Sandy for another delicious meal, she went to her bedroom, climbed into the recliner and pulled her phone from her pocket.

"Hi Joanne, Kate here. How are you both doing?"

"Good to hear your voice. We are both fine, and your house is still in one piece. We've been out most days hunting for something to rent. We have gone as far as Chatham to the west and Tillsonburg to the east. There seems to be a shortage of rentals. I guess we're spoiled after enjoying your home."

"That's why I called. Gran asked me to stay out here for at least another month. To tell you the truth, she'd like me to stay out here permanently to oversee the investment of her money into various charities. I don't feel I have the experience necessary to do that, but she is insisting, so I agreed to try it for one month. If it works out, I might get a teaching job here, or try my hand at writing Children's Literature. Dana and I went to a conference and we're eager to collaborate on a book. Would you have any objection to house-sitting for a while?"

"We'd be thrilled to stay here. If a rental becomes available in the meantime, I'll contact you. I know the Lord has always provided for our needs, and for some reason, he still wants us in your house. We are enjoying lettuce and radishes from the garden. There will be a good crop of tomatoes from the plants your Father put in. They are green, of course, but growing bigger every day."

"As you know, I came out here to get closure on my parents' deaths. I met with the coroner, the police officer, the lawyer for the young man and the young man himself. I now believe that the Lord called Mom and

Dad home through this accident. Grief still hits me at the most unexpected times, but I see God's plan in all this. The anger is definitely going as I accept what I cannot change and pray.

"Has Stuart bothered you anymore?"

"Not since Mr. Howet had his secretary deliver a letter to him a few days ago warning him that if it continued, I'd get him charged with harassment. Unfortunately, Mr. Howet died. They suspect that he was killed, but the investigation is ongoing."

"I read something about his death in the local paper. How terrible for his wife. We will keep her in our prayers."

"Thank you again for keeping an eye on the house."

"It's our pleasure. It sounds like the Island has been a good place for you to heal emotionally after your tragedy. Goodbye for now."

Later that afternoon, while Kate and Lily were in the quilting room, they spotted Jerry and Bill pushing two wheelbarrow loads of branches up to the pit in the middle of the backyard. Then after half an hour, they were back with two more loads of twigs and bark.

Kate and Lily took a break from their projects and walked toward the pit.

"Where did all the branches come from?" Lily asked.

"Was windy overnight, and it shook the loose branches out of the trees. You have enough now for a wiener roast," Bill said with a chuckle. "Jerry has been a great help today."

"I'm learning a lot from Bill," Jerry said as he turned and smiled at Bill. "A property this size requires much more knowledge and skill to maintain than a regular backyard."

"I'll tell Sandy that we'll roast wieners tomorrow for lunch. It's been years since we had a wiener roast, and nothing tastes as good as one roasted over a fire," Lily said.

The buzzer sounded, announcing a car at the gate. Lily went back inside while Kate helped to pick up some small branches that had scattered. Paul was on the intercom and asked if he might speak privately to Lily for a few minutes. Once inside, Lily took him to her bedroom, and they sat on the recliners.

"Lily, I got the results back from the University of California. According to scientists there, the samples are a match. The woman in the locket is my biological mother."

"How do you feel about that, Paul?"

"I've thought about nothing else since I found the locket a couple of weeks ago. I have so many questions. I wish I knew who she was, why she gave me up, whether she chose my parents, and who was my biological father. I'm still confused, but at least one part of the puzzle is in place. Thank you again, Lily, for making it possible."

"I was only too happy to help. Now, we have to get the other information collected. I've used a Private Investigator in the Burlington area and he's been most helpful. The envelope you found the locket in had

McMaster University stamped on one corner. With your permission, I'd like to ask Garth to initiate a search to get information that could answer your questions. You'll need to send the picture of your mother to him over your cell phone."

"I want to reimburse you for any expenses, Lily. You've already been more than generous. Also, since my parents who raised me were not my biological parents, I hope I can assume that Alzheimer's doesn't run in my family. That being the case, I'll take you up on your offer to help with the charities and work with Kate."

"Well, well, well," Lily said with a smile. "The Lord does work in mysterious ways. Another answer to my prayers."

After hugging Lily and thanking her for helping him unravel the mystery, he left, promising to send the picture to Garth. Lily headed for the phone on her nightstand and got hold of Garth.

"Garth, Lily here."

"Hi Lily. What are you up to now?"

"I have a young friend named Paul Moffet, who recently had a DNA test done to see if some hair in a locket was his biological mother's hair. He just got word that it is a match, so now we need to locate the mother. He was born on Aug. 13, 1996. He found an envelope with writing on the front that said,

'For my child when it is time.

Tell my child that I love him or her with all of my heart. The locket is to be a reminder of my love. God Bless You.'

"The note is not signed. On the corner of the envelope is a stamp that says McMaster University.

"The locket has a picture of a young woman on one side and hair on the other. I've asked Paul to send the picture to you on his cell phone. I'm afraid there isn't much to go on."

"I'll start at McMaster University. There is a hospital connected to the University. That could be where she gave birth. I'll begin right away. If it was a private adoption, it'll be harder to locate her. This could be wrapped up quickly if she went through a public agency. I'll also try the adoption registries once we have a name. Maybe she is searching for him, too.

"By the way, the police detective I know in St. Thomas told me they are looking for Stuart. They have evidence that he was in Mr. Howet's office recently. I told them about the conversation I overheard in the hallway, and they are speaking with his employer. Stuart has not been seen since he left the office in a huff. He hasn't returned to his apartment, or had contact with his clients."

"Do they think he killed Mr. Howet?" Lily asked.

"They're calling him a person of interest. Since we don't know where he is, tell Kate to be careful. Bye, for now, Lily."

chapter twelve

While Sandy got the patio table set and made a tossed salad with orange dressing to have with the wieners, Bill got some kindling and started a fire. The smell of the wood brought back camp memories for Kate. Sensing movement overhead, she tilted her head so she was looking skyward. A bald eagle was gliding as though it was riding an air current with its huge wings stretched out horizontally. As Kate continued to watch, she saw it descend to a large Douglas Fir tree not far from the house. After dinner, she planned to get closer to the tree to see if it had a nest.

Bill and Kate speared wieners on each of two sticks and proceeded to roast them. They both had fits of laughter as their stomachs gurgled, anticipating the meal. Sandy and Lily were already on comfortable chairs at the table, enjoying the light breeze that kept the day from being too hot. As soon as the wieners were done, Sandy slipped them into the lightly toasted buns and everyone dove into the condiments. For many minutes there was no sound except for a symphony of bird calls while the wieners were thoroughly enjoyed.

"Why does food always taste better when you eat it outside?" Sandy asked.

"Maybe because nature encourages us to relax and appreciate it more," suggested Bill as he licked a glob of mustard off his thumb.

After chatting about nothing in particular, but enjoying each other's company, they all rose from the table to clean up and ensure that the fire was properly extinguished.

"Just before we all go our separate ways, I want you to be aware of something that could pose a danger. Someone from Ontario has been harassing Kate. This individual is now wanted by the police as a person of interest in connection with a death there. At this point, his whereabouts are not known. While he is probably still in Ontario, he might have headed for Vancouver Island. Please do not automatically open the gate giving access to a car until you know who it is. If the name Stuart Coghill is given, do not open the gate and call the police. We have been advised to be careful and more alert than usual," Lily explained.

Everyone, including Kate, stood in shock at this announcement. It was like a beautiful day, a delicious dinner, good company and stunning nature had suddenly been overshadowed by a dark cloud. "Gran, how do you know this?" Kate asked in disbelief.

"Garth told me. He got the information from his friend on the St. Thomas Police Force."

"Do you have a picture of Stuart Coghill so we can recognize him?" Bill asked, looking concerned.

Both Kate and Lily shook their heads. Then Kate got an idea. Taking out her phone, she searched for the realty office in St. Thomas. Sure enough, there was a picture of him. "Here's his picture."

As they dispersed, Lily to have an afternoon nap, Sandy to clean up the kitchen and Bill to tidy the patio, concerns and fears were foremost in their thoughts. Kate went immediately to get her Bible. Sitting on the porch, she looked up one of her favourite verses for times when she felt her life was out of control. 'Hide not thy face far from me; put not thy servant away in anger: thou hast been my help; leave me not, neither forsake me, O God of my salvation. When my father and my mother forsake me, then the Lord will take me up.' (Psalm 27:9,10) After reading the verses several times, a feeling of peace came over her. If Kate looked at her circumstances, she would panic. If she looked to God, she had the assurance that she was in his care and he'd be with her.

Kate spent the afternoon exploring Lily's property, following the many trails and appreciating the beautiful rhodo bushes that were a mass of blooms. A walk through nature had a healing quality for her. Kate thought about the first garden and wondered what the Garden of Eden had been like before Adam and Eve sinned.

After dinner, while sitting on the porch, she heard Sandy and Bill leaving. She assumed Gran was probably close to retiring for the night. From where she was seated, Kate spotted the eagle once again, cruising toward the same tree. Even though it was dusk, Kate thought she could still spot a nest in the tree if she got close enough. She was at the base of the tree, peering straight up through the branches when something that felt like a red-hot needle went into her foot. Looking down, she saw a giant hornet on her foot. Using her other foot, she kicked it and in doing so, it struck the ground. Grabbing a tissue from her pocket, she scooped it up. It was obviously dead, but her foot was swelling quickly to twice the size, and the pain was getting more extreme by the second. Kate kicked off her shoe, limped back up to the house, slid open the patio doors, and yelled for Lily. She sat on the closest chair, her foot out in front of her, and tears streamed down her face from the excruciating pain and throbbing. Lily, fortunately, had not yet retired for the night and heard the scream for help.

"Oh, my!" exclaimed Lily looking at Kate's foot.

"Gran, the pain is awful. I don't think I can stand it!" whimpered Kate, clutching her lower leg.

"What caused it to swell so much?" asked Gran.

"It was the biggest hornet I've ever seen. I wrapped it in a tissue in my pocket. But I really need something for the pain."

"Kate, I'm worried you might be allergic to hornet stings, which can be serious. We need to have you checked out at the hospital. I can't drive at night with my old eyes and you certainly can't drive. I'm going to call Paul."

Reaching for the closest phone in the kitchen, Lily dialled Paul's number, and he picked up on the first ring. She explained her concerns, and Paul assured her he would be there immediately. Before returning to the kitchen, Lily pressed the button to open the gate and grabbed Kate's purse from the hook in the front hall. Slowly and in excessive pain, Kate and Gran made it to the front door just as Paul pulled up in his car. Within seconds, she was seated with her foot extended, and they were racing down the highway to the hospital in Nanaimo. Lily went inside, pushed the button to close the gate, and laid on the living room sofa while praying for Kate.

Paul sensed Kate was trying her best to hide the pain, but with her foot continuing to swell, and turning beet red in the centre, he concluded this was no normal bite. Any attempts at conversation resulted in one-word answers as though even talking added to her discomfort. Over the years, he had made numerous trips to the hospital but never as quickly as this evening.

Upon their arrival, Kate swung her legs out, while Paul grabbed a wheelchair at the emergency entrance.

Within seconds of arriving, Kate was taken to a separate cubicle to wait for the attending physician to make his appearance, which couldn't be soon enough for her. Paul settled himself in the waiting room and prayed for Kate and that the doctor would have the skill to help her. He had wanted to accompany her, but he respected the fact that he didn't have the right to do so. Paul prayed that someday he would have the right to be at her side. He wanted to let her know he thought she was special, but he wasn't sure she was ready to hear that after Stuart.

A tall, thin doctor in his mid-forties entered the room. "Hi. I'm Dr. McDowell. Let's have a look at your foot. Tell me what happened."

"I was outside, peering up at an eagle's nest, when suddenly I felt something like a red-hot poker plunge into my foot. The pain is awful."

"What did this insect look like?"

"I killed it with my other foot. It's in my pocket in a tissue," Kate said as she extricated it from her pocket and handed it to Dr. McDowell.

"Nurse, would you please get a couple of ice packs and a Tylenol three?"

Turning back to Kate after looking at the hornet, he said, "You were stung by a Murder Hornet, as they call them on the Island here. Their official name is Japanese Hornet. They're rare because they're not natural to Vancouver Island. I had one case last year, but people have also been stung on the mainland at White Rock and Vancouver. Their venom is seven times more toxic than a regular hornet, and they're capable of giving multiple stings. You're very fortunate to get only one sting. Some people in Japan have died from multiple stings. I suggest you keep the hornet because I'll have to report this to the Invasive Species Council of BC. They'll probably contact you and want to come to your property to search for a nest, usually under a tree, or in a hole in the tree trunk.."

"How do you think it got here?" Kate asked as the nurse returned with the ice and the pill.

"Probably on a cruise ship or a cargo boat. Who brought you in tonight?"

"Paul, a friend of mine. He's out in the waiting room."

As Kate was taking the pill, the doctor arranged the ice over her severely swollen foot, all the while humming.

"That's one of my favourite songs," Kate said.

"It's a habit of mine. Ever since I was a child, I've loved to hum and sometimes I don't realize I'm doing it. Amazing Grace is a favourite of mine as well. The words describe me to a tee," said Dr. McDowell as he took another look at her foot.

"I'll be back in just a minute. The pill should start to reduce the pain in about twenty minutes, but don't be surprised if it doesn't entirely leave for a few days."

The Doctor returned with Paul, who he recognized as the Chaplain.

"I recommend you stay in the hospital for at least an hour. If an allergic reaction is going to occur, it should happen by then. The pain won't feel quite as acute if you get your mind off it, so I suggest that Paul give you a tour of the hospital in the wheelchair. If you feel faint, breathless, can't swallow or the swelling seems to be going up your leg, return here immediately. Here are a few more Tylenol three tablets. I think you'll need them for a couple of days," said Dr. McDowell as he handed Kate the pills and moved on to the next patient.

"Let's start with a happy floor," Paul said, as he wheeled her onto the elevator.

When the elevator doors slid open, Kate knew immediately where they were. "For being a happy floor, as you call it, there's a lot of loud crying."

As they stopped and looked at the babies, each in their own little crib, Paul looked down at Kate.

"Did Lily tell you I spoke with her today and shared the results from the maternity test?"

"No. What did it show?"

"You were right. The girl in the photo is my birth mother. I have to wonder why Mom and Dad never told me I was adopted."

"I think they meant to tell you, or why would they have kept the envelope and the locket? They had twenty-six years to throw it away, but they didn't. Try and look at it from their point of view. When would the time be right? When you were a toddler, you were too young to understand. When you started school, you might have felt different from the other kids and wondered why your Mother didn't want you. In high school, you had all kinds of things to deal with emotionally and physically without that bombshell being dropped on you. Probably by the time you graduated from university, they felt they had left it too long, and you would resent them for not telling you sooner. Also, from what Dana told me, they loved you dearly. They might have worried that if you found your birth parents they'd take second place."

"Ya. No time was the perfect time."

The tour through the hospital opened Kate's eyes to the kind of compassionate work Paul was involved in daily. One nurse came up to them and asked Paul to stop in and pray with an elderly gentleman in the Palliative Care Unit who got extremely discouraging news.

Leaving Kate outside the nurses' station, he spoke with the patient. As he exited the room, some ten minutes later, he told Kate that the older man had received a diagnosis of terminal cancer.

"He's afraid to die alone. So we talked and prayed. I promised to come back daily to see him."

An hour later, as they left the hospital parking lot, Kate commented on how kind Dr. McDowell was. "He tried to take my mind off the pain by telling me all about Japanese Hornets. He also did some humming which I think was supposed to cheer me up. I sensed he might be a Christian. He was humming Amazing Grace."

"Our paths don't cross very often. He seems to be stationed in Emergency, and I spend most of my time in Palliative Care. Occasionally, if someone passes away in Emergency, I get paged to help console the family, but Dr. McDowell hasn't been on duty."

There was little conversation on the drive home. Both Paul and Kate seemed to be deep in thought until Paul noticed Kate swiping at her eyes. "Are you in more pain?"

"No. I was just missing my parents. Here I am, twenty-six years old and longing for a hug from my Mom. She was always so kind and caring, which made you feel like she had the healing touch. Sometimes I have the most dreadful feeling of homesickness come over me. I think they call it grief, but this emotional response is exactly like the one I had the first time I went to an overnight camp. You don't miss the physical house you live in, but rather the precious people who live there."

"I can relate to your experience, Kate. When my parents died in a boating accident last year, there were times when I felt a wave of grief hit me. Sometimes it hit when I entered the house, and there was no cheery greeting, no one asking how my day had gone. Other times it was when I was watching a hockey game on TV, and Dad wasn't there telling the players what they needed to improve on. He gave them a lot of advice they never heard," Paul said, with a grin. "Every sailboat I see out on the ocean brings back memories of them waving to me on shore. They ended up with a kid who didn't like water. Right from the time I was a baby, I didn't like it. Even if it was just the bathtub, I would holler and shriek."

"Yet, you learned how to swim."

"Oh, yes! My parents didn't force me to go out on the boat, but they were adamant that I learn to swim for my own safety."

"What did you do while they were boating?"

"I spent a lot of time with Bob, the retired gentleman who lived next door. His wife died several years ago, and he was lonely. He had a woodworking shop out back and that was my second home. Bob taught me everything I know about working with wood, and I love creating projects using my carpentry skills.

"It sounds like you had a very happy childhood with wonderful parents."

"I didn't realize it at the time, but they were the best," Paul agreed.

Paul turned off the Old Island Highway and the gate was just ahead. He braked and exited the car to push the buzzer. A few seconds later, the gate opened, and they could see the house lit up and Lily standing in the doorway. Paul drove up to the front door and then ran to open the car door for Kate. Taking her elbow, he tried to help balance her as she made a real effort not to put weight on the swollen foot. Then unexpectedly, he wrapped his arms around her in a giant bear hug. "I'm not your Mom but I care too."

"Thanks," Kate said, stunned by his actions.

After getting Kate safely inside and answering all of Lily's questions, Paul hugged Lily goodbye and left for home.

"Well, it is past our bedtime, dear. Do you want a snack before retiring?"

"No. The pain has taken my appetite away. I'll be fine until morning, Gran."

"Use my elevator to get to your bedroom. Much easier than the stairs. Try to have a good sleep, Kate."

Before slipping under the covers, Kate put the dead hornet that was still in her pocket out on the dresser where it would be safe in case someone from the Invasive Species Council wanted to see it. She couldn't help but think about Paul too. It had felt so comforting when he held her in that hug, and he had been considerate all evening, anticipating what he could do to make things easier for her. She hated to admit it but she was developing feelings for him. She couldn't help but wonder how he felt about her, especially after her outburst about missing her Mother. The pain pill was making her very dopey. As Kate dropped off to sleep, she hoped she would experience another hug from Paul in the near future.

chapter thirteen

With each passing day, the pain was less intense in Kate's foot, the swelling decreased as well, and she could now fit into a pair of shoes. Putting on socks still made things too tight, but on the whole her foot was healing.

A gentleman from the Invasive Species Council of BC phoned and arranged a visit to examine the insect and the property. The presence of this insect on Vancouver Island was being taken very seriously. As Kate was waiting for his arrival, she went into the quilting room where she had been working on a children's story while Lily cut fabric for another quilt.

"Gran, I think the colour combinations of lime green and mauve are spectacular. What's the pattern you're using?"

" The Wedding Ring," answered Lily. "I chose green

and mauve because this quilt is for a young couple who are getting married, and I wanted to use their favourite colours."

"When is the wedding?"

"They haven't set a date yet, but this quilt has to fit a queen-size bed so it'll take some time to construct."

The buzzing over the intercom signalled the arrival of the gentleman Kate was expecting. Walking out to the front lobby, she pressed the gate button. After introductions were made, she led Mr. Nottingham around to the back of the house where her encounter with the bee had occurred.

"The physician who contacted me mentioned you had the hornet. Could I examine it, please?"

"I have it here," Kate said as she pulled a small plastic bag containing the hornet from her pocket.

"Ah, yes. It's a Japanese Hornet," Mr. Nottingham said as he carefully removed it from the bag with a tiny pair of tweezers. "It still has its stinger in place. You could've been stung several more times. Please show me where you were standing or walking when the attack occurred."

Kate lead the way to the Douglas Fir, where she thought the eagles had a nest.

"I was right about here, gazing up into the tree, looking for an eagle's nest."

"The hornets usually have a nest on the ground under a large exposed tree root. Yes, look here. There is a cavity under this large gnarled root but I don't see any more at the moment."

"For which I'm very thankful," Kate said as she kept an eye on the cavity.

"What time of day were you out here?"

"Around dusk."

"Since I don't see anymore, we'll certainly hope he is a lone invader. But if you should see any, please call us immediately, and we'll do a more thorough search. Here's my card."

"Aside from how painful the sting is, are there any other negative aspects to this creature?" Kate asked.

"Oh yes. The honeybees have no defence against this hornet, and they can kill a colony in just a few hours. Bees are already at risk from pesticides, and we don't want to see them wiped out. They not only provide honey, but they are important for pollination. Fortunately, the Japanese Hornet can't survive our winters, but ships pass here all the time, and they can be unwelcome stowaways."

After Mr. Nottingham left with the hornet in his possession, Kate returned to the quilting room to see Lily relaxing in an easy chair, enjoying the view outside.

"There is something to be said for sitting behind glass when those hornets are around," Lily said.

"He couldn't see anymore, and he thinks this one probably hitched a ride on a ship," Kate explained.

"Gran, you mentioned you had a nurse for Grandfather and she stayed on with you, but I haven't seen her since I arrived."

"When Martha knew you were coming, she asked if

I would mind if she went to Penticton for a couple of weeks to visit with her daughter. Her daughter was expecting a baby a week ago, and she hoped to be there when the baby was born. Martha was boarding the plane just as her daughter went into labour and fortunately, Martha arrived in time."

"That's cutting it close," Kate said.

"I phoned her and explained that you were staying on for a month so there was no rush for her to return. Martha thought I sounded a lot perkier on the phone, and I told her it was because I had two delightful girls visiting with me. I got on the scales this morning and I've gained five pounds. See what a positive effect you've had on me, dear."

"Gran, I was thinking last night about how important it is to forgive. Suppose I had decided I wouldn't forgive you, and had stayed in St. Thomas for the summer and never came out here. So many miraculous things wouldn't have happened. I would've missed out on the blessings God wanted me to have. If we hadn't forgiven Jerry, and instead let the courts work things out, or insisted he be charged, a young man's life could have been ruined."

"The day before Al died, he asked me to forgive him. I admit part of me didn't want to. But I had just asked God to forgive all my sins, which I know he did, so how could I refuse to forgive your Grandfather? Do you remember in the Bible when the disciples asked how many times they must forgive and the Lord said seventy times seven? Well, I think I've finally figured out what that means. When someone hurts us badly, we might forgive them today, but tomorrow we might be thinking about what they did, and the same bitter feelings come to the surface. So, we need to forgive them again and again and again. As long as our memory or the devil brings up the hurt, we must respond with forgiveness. It doesn't mean we are saying what they did is okay. It means we'll obey God's word and leave everything up to him. It's a great feeling to know you don't have to get revenge or make someone pay. God is their judge."

"Every time I hear Stuart's name mentioned, I have to turn the whole awful mess over to God. Sometimes, I don't think he will ever be out of my life."

Later that afternoon, as Kate was missing Dana, her phone rang.

"Hi, I was just thinking about calling you," Kate said, as she answered the phone.

"Oh, I miss you guys so much and the Island too," Dana whined. "What's new with you and Lily?"

"A few days ago, I got stung by a Japanese Hornet and your cousin kindly drove me to the hospital."

"Ouch, sounds painful. Where were you stung?"

"My foot and you should have seen how it swelled up. It resembled a football. Between the swelling and the pain, I couldn't drive myself, nor could Lily with her night blindness. She decided to contact Paul."

"Paul has always been someone you can count on when you need help. Even from the time he was a kid. I remember when we found a raft in the creek near my house. I wanted to take it down the creek, but Paul said he didn't think it was safe, so he wouldn't get on. I figured he just didn't like water. Anyways, the raft and I took off down the creek, but I couldn't get it to stop. Paul found a rope which he threw out to me, and I jumped off the raft and he pulled me towards shore. I had a rope burn for a while, but I was basically in one piece."

"Did he tell you the DNA from the hair proves the girl in the picture is his mother?" asked Kate.

"Yes, he called me a few nights ago and said Lily kindly offered to help him find out who she is and where she lives. I can't believe no one in our family ever knew about this. I guess every family has its secrets. I've another reason for calling. When I talked with Paul, he mentioned that his lawyer friend, Mike Harding, was going crazy trying to hire a legal secretary. They are in short supply on Vancouver Island. Paul mentioned I was a legal secretary and Mike asked Paul to feel me out and see if I was interested. I prayed about it and we had an interview over the computer. The job seems to be a fit. Mike impressed me as being a lot like Mr. Howet, and you know I love Vancouver Island. Mike asked the usual interview-type questions and offered me the job. I told him I'd have to pray about it, and I think the Lord has opened that door for me at just the right time. Mrs. Howet sold the firm to a woman, and she was in two days ago to set the stage for her takeover. She told me that if anyone called with a sob story and wanted pro bono work, just hang up on them. Mr. Howet did all kinds of work for needy people and didn't charge them. The following day, when she arrived, she told me my services wouldn't be needed after Friday because her sister would assume the role of a legal secretary. So the job offer from Mike came at just the right time. Mind you, there are many jobs in my field in Ontario, but sometimes a change is good."

"Wow! I'm thrilled you're returning and wait until Lily hears the good news. You are welcome to stay here."

"I would love to stay with you until I'm sure Mike and I work well together. If everything goes smoothly, I can hunt for an apartment. I'm not planning to sublet my apartment in St. Thomas yet. I don't want to burn bridges, and since Mike wants me there in a few days, I don't have time to pack my stuff and rent storage."

"Let me know when your plane arrives and I'll pick you up in Comox. This is the best news!"

"By the way, the police are still looking for Stuart, and they have contacted the Vancouver Island RCMP to be on the lookout. This morning, an officer came to check on something at the back of the building. They have proof that Stuart was here the night when Mr.

Howet was working late. Do be careful, Kate, in case he's headed your way."

"If he comes here, I'll introduce him to a Japanese Hornet, and that'll put an end to his visit."

"Talk with you soon. Bye for now," Dana said with a chuckle.

A look of concern passed across Kate's face. Stuart was intruding in her life again. Bowing her head, she once more prayed that God would protect her and that the authorities would find Stuart before he did anything else to hurt someone. Kate hoped she wasn't putting Gran at risk by staying with her. Stuart knew she was coming to the Island but not the exact location. Hopefully, he would never find out. As she returned to the house, Kate saw Paul walking toward her. He was proving to be a good friend, and someday if she was honest with herself, she hoped for more. He wasn't stunningly handsome like Stuart but rather good-looking in a wholesome way. His blond hair, muscular build, and moral character made him much more desirable than Stuart ever was.

"Have you heard from Dana?" he asked with a grin.

"Yes, she called earlier. You must be as excited as I am to have her return."

"Dana is my favourite cousin, probably because we were born just months apart. When my parents died, I felt like an orphan with no family nearby. Now with Dana on the way, that will change. Thanks for letting her stay with you and Lily. You have both been so kind to her."

As they neared the house, Kate was concerned to see Lily talking with Officer Hagen, who she had spoken with shortly after arriving on the Island. As they got nearer, the officer turned and smiled at her.

"Officer Hagen just stopped in to speak with us, Kate. Paul, please stay and join us."

Looking tall and handsome in his uniform, Officer Hagen waited for Kate and Paul to get seated.

"I'm so glad to see you again, Kate. I didn't know if you would still be here. I received orders to come out and speak with your Grandmother this morning. We have received word from St. Thomas Police that they have reason to believe Stuart Coghill is on his way out here. It's strongly suspected from the evidence collected so far that he was responsible for Mr. Howet's death. Kate, could you explain why he might be coming this way to see you?"

"I dated him for a few months and he was a charming, attentive companion. Then, when my parents died, he became controlling and demanding. He had some crazy idea that I had inherited money and property, and I should use it to partner with him in a realty business. I explained I couldn't touch my parents' savings or sell the house for a year according to the will. I also told him in no uncertain terms that our relationship was over and not to contact me. However, he kept calling and texting and was increasingly demanding. Finally, I phoned Mr. Howet, and we decided he'd deliver a letter to warn Stuart that if he continued to contact me, I'd have no option but to press harassment charges. I guess he's coming to demand what he cannot have, or because he's very angry with me and I'm his target."

"Did you delete the texts you received from him?"

"No, Mr. Howet advised me not to. You are welcome to read them on my phone," Kate said as she pulled her phone out of her pocket and reached across the table.

After reading for several minutes, Officer Hagen looked up at Kate.

"Mr. Howet gave you good advice. Now I'm going to give you some. I'd like you and your Grandmother to move out of this house until we know where he is. Two women in a house by themselves on a property this size makes you a sitting duck for a man like Coghill."

"Officer Hagen, I appreciate your concern, but we don't even know if he's headed here for sure. What evidence do you have that he killed Mr. Howet?" Kate asked.

"The car he drove that night has specks of brown paint on it. The building Mr. Howet was working in was spray painted at the back from seven until nine. The painters saw a white car like the one he was driving enter the empty parking lot, and they stopped spraying when they noticed it because it was windy, and they were afraid paint would end up on the car. There was a little brown paint on a suit coat in his cupboard and forensics found it matched what was on the building. A security camera in front of the building caught the car and licence plate number. No other cars entered the parking lot that night. Mr. Howet was working on legal concerns for two clients involving Mr. Coghill, which would have adversely affected his livelihood. The fact that he appears to be on the run would indicate he has something to hide."

"Kate didn't tell him she was visiting me," Lily said. "I have two landscapers who are here during the day as well as a housekeeper. I don't think he'll try anything. Also, I can hire a security person overnight if you think it's necessary."

Paul immediately spoke up. "I can drive here after work and sleep on the sofa in the living room. The ladies won't be alone."

"You see, Officer, we are well taken care of. Also, as Christians, we're in the Lord's hands," Kate added.

I'm afraid He outranks the RCMP," Lily said as she smiled at Paul.

"I know it's a real inconvenience to leave your home, but I want to make sure you understand the seriousness of this situation. If you are determined to stay, I'll try and send out a patrol car periodically to buzz you on the intercom from the gate and make sure all is well. If you need help, don't hesitate to call 911. Before I leave, I'd like to forward these texts to our computer at the station as evidence, if I have your permission, Kate."

"That's fine."

It seemed a plan was in place to keep them safe if Stuart was coming to the Island. So Paul left to go home and pack some things he'd need. Once again, they didn't understand what was happening, but their lives were in a state of upheaval because of the evil in someone's heart. They knew God loved them and had a plan, even if it wasn't evident.

chapter fourteen

The night passed without incident and another day lay like a blank page before them. Sandy's arrival to start breakfast had a way of waking the whole house in eager anticipation of what she was making. So far, the threat of Stuart's arrival had not diminished their appetites, so they all arrived at the table thankful indeed for her skill in cooking. Before they began eating, Paul led them in a prayer for safety and to be wise about the need for caution. He also prayed for Stuart, that he would find God's love and turn from the life that he was presently living. As he finished the prayer, the buzzer at the gate sounded, and an officer spoke over the intercom system, asking if they required any assistance.

After assuring him they were fine, Paul left for his duties at the hospital. Kate's phone rang and although she didn't recognize the name or number on the screen, she answered it.

"This is Greg Daniels. I'd like to speak with Kate Grayson, please."

"Speaking," Kate said.

"I've been on the Island since yesterday inspecting the car that your parents were driving at the time of their death. The forensic team, a representative from Transportation and Safety Canada and I have gone over every square inch of the front portion of the car in an attempt to figure out why the airbags did not inflate when the crash occurred. We concluded they were installed backwards. We contacted the manufacturing plant where I work, and they checked several other cars assembled on the same day to ensure this was not a problem. So far, this is the only one. I'd like to stop by today to discuss damages with you."

"We plan on being here all day, so whatever is convenient for you is fine with us," Kate said. After giving him directions, Kate returned to the sewing room to continue editing the children's story she had finished writing. Bill and Jerry passed by the window, seemingly intent on checking the doors and looking for unlocked windows. Lily had mentioned Officer Hagen's visit at breakfast, and Bill had assured her they would stay closer to the house, and have their cell phones with them at all times in case of a problem. Kate couldn't help but think she was responsible for everyone being on high alert. And what if Stuart discovered where she was, and as a result, one of the people she cared for was hurt? Finding it impossible to concentrate on her story, Kate went in search of Lily.

Lily was in her bedroom, sitting in her favourite recliner, looking out the window.

"Hi, Gran. Anything interesting out there?"

"I'd say ugly was a better word," answered Gran. "Every year I see those disgusting-looking green slugs along the trails and marvel at their size."

"I saw them when I was out walking yesterday and I meant to ask you about them."

"The slimy green ones are native to Vancouver Island and are beneficial. The black ones are invasive and can be destructive. After a moment of thought, Gran added, "I guess they are a lot like people. Some have a positive effect on those around them and others are harmful. We usually can't tell which kind we are dealing with by their outward appearance."

"You are so right," agreed Kate, thinking of how Stuart's outward appearance presented a well-put-together young man, but inwardly he was like the black slug—harmful.

Later that morning, Mr. Daniels arrived to discuss the issue of the airbags that didn't inflate. Gran invited him to follow her to the back porch and have a seat. "You have a magnificent view of the Georgia Strait. I can feel my stress level decline just looking at that tranquil water with the mountains towering in all their rugged strength."

"Do you have a stressful job, Mr. Daniels?" Lily inquired.

"Yes, it involves a lot of troubleshooting. We manufacture thousands of cars annually, and while most of them exit our facility in perfect condition, there are always a few with problems. As long as human beings are involved in the process, there will be mistakes. No one is infallible. I'm expected to investigate and try to get to the root of the problem so it doesn't happen again. On behalf of our company, we're so very sorry for your recent losses."

"Thank you," Kate responded.

"When it was discovered that they were installed backwards, our inspector at the plant notified the supervisor of the workers on the assembly line. We believe it was a human error, and the company has considered firing the worker responsible. His union is fighting it on compassionate grounds. His wife has been hospitalized with cancer, and he has four children under ten years of age. They claim he has been under a tremendous amount of stress. His record has been spotless until now. I'm sure you have probably discussed this with your lawyer and I'm authorized to present an offer to you. Anything we discuss here will be shared with our lawyers, and they will contact your lawyer as we move forward."

"My lawyer already informed me that we have grounds for a lawsuit when he was here the other day on another matter," said Lily. "My Granddaughter and I have discussed this, and there are a couple of things we would like to see done instead of a cash settlement. We have asked the city to straighten that bend in the road, put up a large sign with a blinking light indicating a deer crossing, and reduce the speed limit. We'd like your company to put in a roadside stop area for motorists, back from the road about thirty or forty feet as a kind of memorial to my son and daughter-in-law. It would consist of a large raised garden with a stainless steel sign in the middle that would read, 'This garden and rest stop are in memory of Matt and Becky Grayson, who were hit by an oncoming truck that swerved to avoid colliding with two deer. The young man who hit them constructed this garden, and the company which produced the car that had faulty airbags paid for the materials. All are forgiven. In honour of them, search your heart and forgive someone today.'

"We would like a picnic table and an outhouse at the rest stop. It needs to be landscaped with flowering plants and shrubs so there is colour all year round. The cost for everything involved as well as ongoing maintenance, will be the responsibility of your company."

"I'll be honest with you. No one has ever requested something like this before. Usually, they demand a very significant cash settlement."

"I have not discussed my next expectation with Kate because it just came to mind as you were speaking with us. If Kate disagrees with what I'm about to say, she's free to speak her mind. I want you to give the worker, who installed the airbags backwards, an extended leave with pay to be with his family during this difficult time. Under no circumstances is he to be fired or demoted. You must also let him know we forgive him and we're praying for his family."

"I agree with Gran. If your company does not agree to everything, then we will be forced to go the legal route. We want whatever decision they make in writing with all the details laid out plainly and please fax it to us within a week."

"I don't foresee anybody objecting to this settlement," Mr. Daniels said with a grin. "Ladies, I'm not what most people would call a religious man, but I do believe I've met two women today who not only call themselves Christians but actually walk the talk. It's been a pleasure to meet you. Just one more question before I go. If the worker wants to know who was responsible for his extended leave, can I share your name?"

"Yes," Lily said, "But make it plain to him that it was the Lord who gave me the idea."

"Right, you are. Goodbye ladies," Mr. Daniels said as he rose and walked around the house toward his car. If Mr. Daniels had turned around, he would have seen Lily and Kate holding hands and with heads bowed, praying for the worker's family and Mr. Daniels.

The following morning, after spending time doing her devotionals and praying, Kate checked her cell phone. The text said Dana was arriving on the West jet plane from London. She'd be in Comox by 11:30 Pacific time and could Kate pick her up? Kate immediately texted back and rushed down the stairs to tell Lily and Paul, who had already started their breakfast.

"Paul, are you sure you are sleeping okay on the couch?" Kate asked. "There are lots of empty bedrooms upstairs."

"I'm amazingly comfortable," answered Paul. "Anyway, I'm more likely to notice movement or hear an intruder if I'm on the main level. I wonder if there's been any sign of Stuart on the Island. Maybe he never even left Ontario. I'm glad the police are regularly checking in with you throughout the day to ensure everything is peaceful and you don't need assistance."

Lily insisted Kate drive her car to the airport. As she got to the spot where her parents were hit, a wave of grief once again engulfed her. In order to regain her composure, Kate turned her eyes toward the ocean, and concentrated on the beautiful day, and how blessed she was to be on the Island. The trip had taken a little longer than Kate anticipated. She hoped Dana wasn't tired of waiting for her.

Pulling up to the airport terminal, she spotted her friend dressed in Bermuda shorts and a bright pink t-shirt. She was talking to an RCMP officer who Kate recognized as Officer Hagen. Kate pulled up to the curb and exited the car. Dana spotted her first and rushed over with a bear hug. Kate couldn't help but think that the Moffet family really knew how to make people feel cherished.

Officer Hagen approached, looking more serious than the last time he had visited the house.

"Hello, Kate. Dana Moffet called 911 a few minutes ago to report seeing Stuart Coghill at the airport getting into a dirty white sedan."

"Kate, I couldn't believe my eyes when I walked out here and witnessed him trading keys with a young woman. Stuart got behind the wheel of the white sedan, the engine roared to life, and he exited the parking lot before I could record his license number. The woman looked surprised at his sudden departure. She drove off in a blue sports car."

"I checked with the receptionist at the West Jet desk and he isn't listed on any arrivals," shared Officer Hagen. So I assume they just picked the airport to make the trade. I've asked the airport authorities for the security video. Hopefully, we'll be able to identify this young woman and get the license plate numbers of both vehicles. Now we know Stuart is here, the situation requires you to be alert and vigilant. Until now, we only guessed this was his destination. We've been checking his credit card transactions and bank account to pinpoint his whereabouts. So far, he has been to the bank only once in St. Thomas, on the morning after Mr. Howet was killed, and he withdrew everything in cash. He only had twenty-five hundred dollars. He hasn't used his credit cards or debit cards at all. Stuart has probably been paying cash for meals and lodging so we couldn't trace his movements. If Dana hadn't spotted him, we wouldn't have known he was on the Island for sure."

"Wow, Dana, your feet barely landed on this Island and you're already working with the RCMP," Kate said, trying to make light of a situation that was scaring her.

"I only saw him once at the office but I'd know him anywhere. I have a good memory for faces. If my new legal secretary job doesn't work out, maybe I could train with the RCMP," laughed Dana.

"I assume you're staying with Kate, but I'll need your cell phone number in case we require more help identifying this woman. She might come up on our computer with face recognition if she was caught on the surveillance video. If not, I might need you to look through some mugshots."

"I start work at Harding Law Office on Monday," Dana said.

"Just another reminder to be alert at all times and try not to go out by yourselves, especially at night. We will continue our patrols, and I'm sure you're tired of hearing the intercom buzzer, but we think Stuart came here intending to contact you, Kate. He has a pattern of harassment, and if he has found out how wealthy your Grandmother is, he'll no doubt have a plan in place to get some money."

"We appreciate the patrols, and Paul has been faithfully staying on the sofa each night like a kind of guard dog. Jerry and Bill, our landscapers, have tried to stay closer to the house to keep an eye out. And of course, the Lord is with us wherever we go."

"I'm glad you have a faith that strengthens you during times of trial. I couldn't do my job without the Lord," Officer Hagen added.

As Officer Hagen reentered the airport terminal to see if the surveillance video was ready to be viewed, Dana and Kate piled Dana's luggage into the trunk and started back for Qualicum Beach.

Dana was hardly seated, when she turned to Kate with a huge smile. "Now, there's a man that I could fall for. He has great looks, he has a job where he protects people and best of all, it sounds like he's a Christian. I think I'll thoroughly enjoy living on this Island."

"Must I remind you that Stuart has great looks, a great job and let on he was a Christian."

"Not every man we meet will be a fake like Stuart. Kate, you've had Paul living at your house for several days. Have you seen anything fake about him?"

"No, Paul's been great. We've been working with Lily and talking about how to help needy people or animals in our community. He's consistently compassionate and caring. He won't accept Gran's offer to pay for the DNA testing or the private investigator. Paul's parents took out a small insurance policy, and he'll be receiving the money from that shortly. He intends to pay her back every cent. Some guys would have taken advantage of her generosity but not Paul."

"Does this mean you see what a truly wonderful

catch is sitting right under your nose?" Dana asked as Kate glanced in her rearview mirror.

"I have feelings for Paul, as much as I tried not to. I even told Gran I thought being single was best. But I'm afraid I'm falling in love. The only thing is, I'm not sure how Paul feels. If he doesn't feel the same way, and I show my feelings for him, I'll be so embarrassed. Working with him will be awkward."

"Loving someone is always a risk. But I think that to risk not having a relationship because you are afraid of being hurt is a much bigger risk," Dana advised.

"I'm so glad you're back, Dana," Kate said as she took another look in the rearview mirror.

"I notice you keep looking behind us. I don't think Stuart would remember me even if he did see me at the airport. He hasn't seen this car so I don't think we could be followed. You joked at the airport, but I can tell this whole thing is getting to you."

"I'm just afraid that because of me, someone I care about will be hurt as collateral damage."

"There is no way this is your fault. Look ahead with hope and leave the rest up to the Lord. You're not in this alone."

As they entered the house encumbered with Dana's suitcases, Kate was grateful for such an understanding friend. Another blessing in God's plan for her.

chapter fifteen

Traffic was particularly heavy as Garth took the exit ramp off Highway 403 to proceed to McMaster Hospital in Hamilton. Over the last few years, he had noticed condos and apartments going up at a rapid rate around the Burlington and Hamilton area. As people moved into this part of the province, it meant more traffic on the roads. For the last ten years, he had thought about moving to a quieter place where life was less hectic. Maybe he just needed a holiday. Garth was very tempted to take Lily up on her kind offer to visit. After parking his Toyota Corolla in the first available parking space, he headed into the hospital, to hopefully get Lily the information she wanted. He sensed a change in her recently when they talked on the phone. She seemed calmer and more interested in other people. Although they had never met, he considered her to be his long-distance friend.

He noticed a large floor plan of the hospital mounted on the wall inside the automatic sliding doors and he quickly figured out where the maternity ward was in relation to where he was presently standing. He exited the elevator on the third floor and saw a nurses' station immediately in front of him.

All of the nurses looked too young to be able to give him information that went back twenty-six years. As he walked down the hall, he spotted a pleasant-looking nurse, probably in her late forties, with some grey hair.

"Excuse me, I'm Garth Ellsworth, a private investigator and I've been hired by an elderly lady on Vancouver Island who wants me to find out as much as possible about a young woman who gave birth here on August 13, 1996. Would you have been nursing here then?"

"Yes, I was," Judy Portus answered. "I'm the oldest nurse in the maternity ward."

"I'm sure you have cared for a lot of patients over the years, but it would be much appreciated if you recognize this young woman," Garth said as he showed her the picture on his phone.

"Yes, I remember her. She came in by herself. She was a beautiful young woman and as we waited for the contractions to get closer, she told me about growing up on the mission field, and the wonderful childhood she experienced. She came to McMaster University to become a nurse. She planned on returning to the mission field to help in the hospital there. I also recall her saying that she wanted her child to have two loving parents like she did, and grow up to love the Lord."

"Do you remember her name?"

"No, I'm sorry. Many young women go through here, and she wasn't here as long as most of them."

"Did she mention where the mission field was?"

"No, I don't remember her saying,"

"Did she tell you who the father of the baby was?"

"I asked about the baby's father. She said she thought they were in love and admitted that they should have waited to be intimate until they were married. Apparently, he didn't want the responsibility for the baby, and she never saw him again after she refused to have an abortion. She told me they were both immature and had a lot of growing up to do. But I'm sorry, I don't remember her ever mentioning his name."

"Would there be a record of it in the hospital on any papers she signed?".

"Possibly but those are considered confidential, so I don't believe you'd be given access to them. I must tell you what a special young lady she was. Some single girls going through labour swear and blame others for their mess. Not this girl. Between contractions, I could tell she was praying. She handed me a brown envelope to be given to the adoptive parents when they came for the baby. After several hours of labour, she delivered the baby, and I told her she had a healthy baby boy. She smiled and signed the birth certificate, but then the hemorrhaging began. She never saw him on this earth, but maybe she has been watching him from afar. The doctor did everything possible to save her. Her death hit me hard. I was a recent graduate and this was the first young person who I'd seen die. The adoptive parents came immediately to get the baby. Love and joy just radiated from this couple. I believe he went to a home where he would be cherished."

"That had to have been a hard day for you," Garth said.

"Yes. The doctor asked me to look up the records for the next of kin. I left a message with someone at the mission station and we eventually got word back that her parents would be in Hamilton as soon as they could get a flight."

"Did she mention where she stayed before coming here?"

"I don't recall her saying anything, but when I was putting her personal effects together to be given to her parents, there was a brochure from the Salvation Army. I noticed it because she had written a Bible Verse in handwriting on top of it. I sent her suitcase and personal items down to the morgue with her body. The Salvation Army has a home for unwed mothers. You might want to try there."

"Thank you for taking the time to talk with me. I'll head there now. But I need to tell you the little boy grew up and is now a Chaplain at a hospital in British Columbia. I'd say the young lady's prayers were answered."

After setting his GPS, Garth followed the oral directions, and within minutes found himself at the Salvation Army's home for unwed mothers. He was greeted by a young woman who was pregnant.

"I need to speak with a staff member who has been here for many years, and worked closely with the girls who stayed here?" Garth requested.

The young woman picked up her phone and asked Josie to come to the front office. A large, motherly-looking woman came down the stairs and approached Garth.

"Hello, I'm Josie. How can I help you?"

"I'm trying to find out who the woman in this photograph is," Garth said as he turned his phone so she could see the picture.

"That's Sarah Smith. I never forget one of my girls. Her name was very common, so it is still in my memory. She was here for about four months leading up to the birth of her baby. We don't usually have our residents stay that long, but Sarah had no family support here and couldn't live at the University over the summer so we made an exception. She worked in the front office like the girl who greeted you when you arrived."

"Did she ever tell you anything about the father?"

"I don't remember him ever coming to see her, or for that matter, I don't think she ever mentioned him."

"I believe her baby was adopted. Do you know how that was arranged?"

"Yes. We work closely with our girls as they decide

whether they should raise the baby on their own, or put the child up for adoption. There is, of course, no right or wrong answer. But we want them to think out their plan carefully. Sarah prayed about her decision and felt it was best for the baby if she put it up for adoption provided she could find a Christian couple who would provide a loving home. The Captain of one of our local citadels had a sister and brother-in-law who had wanted a child for years. She had several miscarriages, and although they saw numerous specialists, a baby never made it to birth. They were active church members in Willowdale and had everyone they knew praying that they would find a baby to adopt. The Captain met Sarah when he came to lead a Bible Study with the girls here. He asked the girls to pray for his sister and brother-in-law. After the Bible Study, Sarah approached him and asked if this couple could come to Hamilton to meet her. He arranged the meeting and Sarah was sure she had met the couple who would love her baby. They seemed to have a strong faith, were obviously in love with each other, and desperately wanted a baby. The adoption was arranged privately. Sarah was to come back here for about a month after the baby was born since her classes at the University didn't start until mid-September. Unfortunately, she died in childbirth. We got to know and love Sarah while she was here and it hit us very hard."

"Are you able to give me the name of the Captain or the adoptive parents?" inquired Garth.

"No, I don't remember the Captain's name and I never met the adoptive parents. It was a private adoption, so no record of it is kept here. In the Salvation Army, the Captains are relocated to a new citadel about every three to five years, so I'm sure he's not still in this area."

"Thank you, Josie. An older lady on Vancouver Island hired me to find out as much as possible about this young woman. She will be very pleased to know that we now have a name. God bless you for the compassionate care you give these girls."

"God bless you too, Garth."

The weekend flew by and Lily realized that having three twenty-six-year-olds in the house, with all the noise and activity they could create, was just what she needed to stay young. She took an afternoon nap to recharge her old batteries while they were off on a jaunt to the beach or sitting on the back porch playing board games which usually ended in mock fights.

Officer Hagen had arrived Sunday afternoon to show Dana some pictures, so Kate and Paul went off together to check out Lily's ten-acre property. When they returned holding hands, Lily reminded herself that she had better get working on that quilt, or it would never be done in time.

Martha, who was back from visiting her daughter, had phoned and invited Kate, Sandy and Lily to go out for lunch with her in Qualicum Beach so she could have an update on how things were going. When she heard Dana was back, she invited her to come as well, but her new job started on Monday so she regretfully declined.

Late Sunday evening, after following a couple of leads that didn't result in more information, Garth took out his notebook and called Lily. Referring to his notes, he told Lily all he had discovered. Lily was pleased to know the girl's name, but disappointed she was no longer on this earth to meet her son. Lily had envisioned a surprise reunion, but that wouldn't be possible. Garth also mentioned he had no success finding out the father's name or locating the Grandparents. Lily asked Garth to continue to search until he ran out of leads or places to look. After spending a few minutes discussing the latest news on Stuart Coghill, they ended their conversation with Garth hinting that he might take Lily up on her offer for him to visit.

Monday morning, Kate woke up with a headache and stomach cramps. Instead of going down for breakfast, she got the heating pad from the ensuite bathroom, took pain medication and crawled back into bed.

Dana knocked on her door as she was leaving for work and Kate asked her to tell Lily that she couldn't go to lunch with them, but would like to meet Martha when they got back. A few hours later, the cramps started to subside, so Kate put on her sweatpants and an old T-shirt. Grabbing a cup of coffee in the kitchen, she opened the sliding doors and settled into a lounge chair on the back porch. Kate thought she heard someone walking along the trail from the other side of the property. Then she remembered that Bill and Jerry often scouted the property and it was probably them. She was almost asleep when she felt her arm being grabbed in a wrench-like hold and found herself being pulled off the chair, pushed off the porch, and propelled along the trail. As she turned to see who was orchestrating this, she saw Stuart's face with a look of pure hate on his features.

"Don't even think about yelling for help. I made sure nobody was around before I grabbed you. Keep moving. For once, you aren't going to ruin my plans."

Kate scanned the woods frantically, hoping to see a way out of this terrorizing situation. She sensed Stuart was seething with anger. Kate never thought him capable of such evil. She felt remaining calm was the best way to get out of this situation alive. But she could feel her pulse racing with every punch Stuart pounded into her back to keep her moving. She prayed God would give her the courage to endure whatever he allowed.

"Stuart, what do you want?" Kate asked, wiping the perspiration off her forehead with her hand.

"I asked myself, why was Kate coming to the Island? I remembered your parents were coming here to see your Grandmother, so I looked up Grayson on the internet, and low and behold, the Graysons are one of the wealthiest families on Vancouver Island. Since you ruined my plans to get my own realty office, it's only fair that you provide the big bucks I'll require to live in luxury. I'm sure your Grandmother has bonded with you by now and will be more than willing to provide a ransom to get you back."

"You want a ransom!"

"Yes, I figure you are probably worth three million dollars," replied Stuart with a sneer as he continued to plunge his fist into Kate's back. It felt like his knuckles were penetrating her skin.

"Stuart, God loves you and has a much better plan for your life. It's not too late to change."

"Cut the religious lingo, Kate. I heard enough of that while I was dating you. You were sweet and compliant until your parents died. I thought your parents' deaths were very fortuitous to my plans, but then you had that meeting with Howet and everything changed."

"Did you kill Mr. Howet?"

"I went there just wanting him to hand over your parents' will, but once again, he wouldn't cooperate. I needed to know what I was up against. He told me I didn't need to worry about getting money for a realty business because I'd be losing my licence over a very clever scheme I had used. That was the last straw. He was ruining my plans. We got into a push-and-shove altercation when I tried to get past him to retrieve the will from his filing cabinet. He lost his footing and hit his head on a ceramic planter. He looked dead to me, so I dragged him to the stairwell and pushed him down the concrete steps to make it look like an accident. I returned to the office and searched the G files for the will. I found the letter they left you and the harassment letter, which I destroyed."

Up ahead, Kate could see a dirty white car, the one Dana had described Stuart getting into at the airport. Bile rose up in her throat as she thought about what could happen to her once he had her trapped in that car. She knew she had to act quickly, but it would be impossible to outrun him wearing flip-flops, and she was exhausted from the repeated blows to her back. Kate realized she was letting fear and panic replace her faith. As soon as she prayed, a sense of peace replaced the fear. Her brain, which had been paralyzed by fear, started functioning. Stuart might think he was in control, but God had her life in His hands. As she was scanning the area, Kate suddenly noticed movement behind the storage shed.

Stuart was probably too busy pounding his fist into her back to notice. She decided to pretend to trip and land on the ground. As she lunged forward, she expected Stuart to grab her arms and yank her to her feet, but instead, she heard scuffling behind her, and when she turned, she saw two muscular RCMP officers holding Stuart's arms and handcuffing him. He was forced to stop thrashing about but his face was red and contorted with anger.

They radioed for a squad car and the ambulance to

proceed down the service road. Both of them had been positioned at the top of the lane. Stuart was placed behind the steel restraining grate in the police cruiser.

Trembling but relieved and thankful, Kate remained on the ground catching her breath. Then, after being checked out by the paramedics, a second squad car drove her down the lane leading to the house and a female officer accompanied her inside. After questioning Kate about Stuart's abuse, the Officer took a picture of her back covered in huge red welts. She explained she couldn't leave her here alone after what she had just experienced. Kate gave her Paul's number. About thirty minutes later, he rushed through the front door and Kate fell into his arms, sobbing. The officer quietly left, assured that Kate had the support she needed.

Paul let her sob for several minutes, knowing from his experience at the hospital that it is better to say nothing and let the victim release the emotional hurt. Finally, her sobs subsided and he led her to the couch, where he sat with his arm around her and her head rested on his shoulder. Paul's breathing was shallow as he came to grips with what had just transpired and how close Kate came to being kidnapped or killed. Little by little, his love for her had grown to the point where he knew his life would be empty without her. But as much as he was tempted to share his heart with Kate, he didn't think she was ready to hear it. Stuart had hurt her and shattered her confidence in herself.

"Do you want to talk about it yet?" Paul asked.

"No. Later. I just want to sit here and feel safe."

An hour later, when the ladies returned from their luncheon, it was to find Paul and Kate sitting on the couch. Kate was covered in dirt from her tripping episode and her mascara was running down her face. Several tissues were crumpled up on the coffee table and Paul's shirt was wet from Kate's sobbing.

"Oh my," Lily said. "What happened?"

"Stuart came calling," Kate answered, still shaken and in pain from the beating.

The ladies quickly found seats and Kate shared her experience. They were all shocked and grateful that Kate hadn't been seriously hurt. Officer Hagen arrived to get a statement from Kate as part of the paperwork filed against Stuart.

"Officer Hagen, I have some questions of my own, now I'm over the shock of what happened. Why were the officers behind that shed?"

"Jerry, your landscaper, was late getting to work this morning because he had a dental appointment. Bill had told him to always use the service road and park on the other side of the property. When he got there, he saw the white car and was suspicious, so he called 911. They forwarded the call to my office. The two closest squad cars responded and used a drone to follow Stuart's movements. The same officers saw him grab you on the porch and shove you along the trail. They decided to leave their cars on the road and come down on foot to hide behind the shed. They didn't know if he was armed because the drone had to stay above the trees. They were in a position to arrest him when you fell. Unknown to you, we've had a drone go over your property twice a day, morning and last afternoon, for the past week to tighten security. Fortunately, there is a video camera attached to the drone, so we have proof of the abduction, and the physical assault on you as he used his fist to plummet you repeatedly. Your groundskeeper was actually very close by, but he was using an electric chain saw to cut long branches, and he didn't hear or see a thing. The first he knew of the incident was when the officer called from her cruiser and asked him to open the gate so she could bring you back to the house."

"What's going to happen to Stuart?" Kate asked.

"He's being transferred in police custody to the Forensic Science Mental Health Facility in St. Thomas to be assessed. He'll probably be charged with manslaughter or second-degree murder and attempted kidnapping at the very least. There might be several more charges as our investigation continues. Our forensic team has already located a new hunting knife hidden under the front seat. They'll be testing it for fingerprints. He'll be off the Island by tonight, and hopefully, you can put this all behind you. Although, when the trial comes up, you could be called as a witness."

"I know he needs a lot of help and I hope he gets treatment," Kate said.

When Dana arrived home from her first day at work and parked Lily's car back in the garage, she was surprised to see everyone still looking shocked as she walked in. After another round of lengthy explanations, Dana and Sandy went into the kitchen to prepare something fast for supper. Creamed salmon on toast with a carrot salad on the side was ready in minutes. Meanwhile, Kate had taken the time to shower and change into her green sweatpants and matching shirt. Paul led them in grace.

"Lord, thank you for your hand of protection over Kate today. Please bless the officers who daily risk their lives to protect us. We pray that Stuart will accept you as his Lord and Saviour, and have a total change in his life. Now, please bless the hands that prepared this food, and nourish our bodies so we can serve you. In Christ's name, we ask this. Amen."

A look of endearment passed between Paul and Kate. No one seemed aware of it as they feasted on the delicious meal. Lily chose to share what Garth had told her at another time. Everyone had experienced enough excitement for one day.

chapter sixteen

At breakfast the next morning, everyone wanted to know if Dana enjoyed her first day on the job. She explained she was on the road a lot, delivering papers to be signed, wills to be mailed, and collecting documents from the courthouse. The work had piled up since Mike Harding's last legal secretary had left three weeks ago. She used his car to run errands, but she needed a car of her own. Kate suggested contacting a moving company to see if they were expecting any moving vans from Ontario. If they were, Dana could request they pick up her car and bring it out.

Lily reminded Dana that she was welcome to use her car until she found a solution to the problem. Still, Dana felt that if she used Lily's car too often, she would be spoiled and unsatisfied with her little runabout. Dana also pointed out how expensive gas was on the Island and her little bug used very little. Until her car arrived, she planned on renting one in Qualicum Beach.

Shortly after Dana left, Lily asked to speak briefly with Paul and Kate in the quilting room before Paul left for the hospital.

"Paul, I heard from Garth yesterday, after his trip to McMaster Hospital and Grace Haven, the Salvation Army Home for unwed mothers. He learned your birth Mother was Sarah Smith and, unfortunately, she died right after she gave birth to you from severe hemorrhaging. I'm so sorry. I had hopes of planning a meeting with your Mother."

"I was optimistic I'd connect with her too, Lily. I had hoped to fill the void left by the death of my adoptive parents, by knowing my birth mother. Someday, I hope to meet her in heaven if she was a Christian."

"Oh, she was. Garth told me her parents raised her on the mission field. She came to McMaster to become a nurse, and she wanted to return to assist in the mission hospital. Your Mother insisted on picking out your adoptive parents herself, and when she met them, she knew they would bring you up in a Christian home. Even when she was in the delivery room, she was praying. She gave the envelope you found to the nurse to pass on to your adoptive parents when they picked you up. You'll most definitely meet your Mom in heaven."

Tears were evident in Paul's eyes as he processed what she was saying.

"Garth hasn't given up on trying to find out who

your Father is or where your Grandparents are living. We can still hope for a reunion if that is part of God's plan."

"Thank you, Lily."

"I've written down Garth's phone number for you if you want to speak with him directly."

"If you don't mind, I'll contact him."

As Kate walked Paul to the door where they hugged, the buzzer sounded on the intercom. It was Martha wanting to talk to Kate. Kate opened the gate and then greeted her at the front door.

"Can we go for a little walk?" Martha asked. With all the excitement yesterday, I didn't get to talk to you."

"Sure, let's sit down by the water," suggested Kate as they made their way along the trail.

"You don't know how glad I am that you came to see your Grandmother. I see such a change in her outlook and emotional state."

"I feel the same way. We've grown very close after just a few weeks. How I wish she'd been part of my life as I was growing up."

"Has Lily said anything to you about her heart condition?" asked Martha.

"No, she doesn't talk about any health problems."

"I'm not trying to alarm you but Lily's heart condition is serious. She should've had bypass surgery years ago. I've gone with her to her doctor appointments for the last few months. The doctor has done all that he can do. A heart attack could happen at any time and probably be fatal. I need to prepare you for what could happen, and we'll pray she has a lot more time with us."

"I had no idea. Just the thought of losing her scares me. Is there anything I should do to help her?"

"Just see she doesn't overtire herself or do anything strenuous. Lily told me she takes an afternoon nap every day, and thankfully, she has a housekeeper and landscapers, so she can do what she enjoys, like quilting."

"Martha, she wants me and Paul to be involved in a kind of trust fund to help charities. I can see it taking more and more of my time as I have to scrutinize them, and then follow up to see that they are using the money appropriately. I'm also writing a children's book, and now Dana is here to do the illustrations, that'll also be time-consuming. If Lily agrees, would you be able to come and stay with her and help Sandy where necessary?"

"Talk it over with Lily and see what she wants. I'd love to do it, but I don't want to intrude if she feels she has enough support. Also, what I do is a form of nursing, but I'm not a registered nurse. I'm a Personal Support Worker, and my role is to go into a home and help patients bathe, do any exercises that have been prescribed, remind them to take their medications and try to keep them from having a fall. I'm paid much less than a nurse, but I love my work. I like to choose the clients I work with, so I haven't signed up with a particular care company. I like to be my own boss."

"Are you married, Martha?"

"My husband died seven years ago. Mike was thirty-five years old. It was a construction accident."

"I'm so sorry," Kate said sympathetically.

"I had to sell the house and move to an apartment. I love to paint Island scenes, but there isn't a lot of inspiration or room to paint. On weekends, I often go for a drive, set up my easel and paint. I enjoy it and it adds to my income. Well, I must be going. I didn't come here to talk about myself."

"I'll get back to you after I speak with Lily. I can tell you care about her, and it would give me peace of mind when I can't be here."

Kate immediately went on a search for Lily. Finding her working on the beautiful mauve and green quilt, she pulled up a chair so Lily could continue quilting while they talked.

"I just chatted with Martha, and I could tell she is very fond of you."

"She told you about my heart condition, didn't she?"

"Yes."

"I wasn't hiding it from you, Kate. I just felt you didn't deserve more bad news. Anyway, I'm feeling fine, and I don't believe in borrowing trouble. I'm so blessed in so many ways that I don't dwell on things I can't change. Someday, when God wants me home, I'll die. I have a heavenly home to look forward to."

"Gran, I'm getting busier by the day with your charity work, which I love doing. Also, now that Dana has arrived, we hope to put the children's book together and get it published. I'll be in and out a lot, and it would ease my mind to know that someone is here with you. Would you consider hiring Martha to be here during the weekdays as a companion?"

"I'm very fond of Martha. She's a peaceful soul. Why don't we ask her if she would consider moving in here? We could offer her room and board and a salary. I want you and Paul to have the freedom to go out, and not have to consider me being here alone," Lily said with a sly grin.

"Wow, what a great idea! Martha said she loves to paint, and she could do that here in this quilting room with you. Gran, there is something else I want to run by you. When you were telling Paul and me about his birth mother this morning, something came to mind. You said her last name was Smith. The couple looking after my house in St. Thomas have the same last name. Now, I know Smith is a common name. You also mentioned her parents were missionaries. Joanne and Don Smith were missionaries. Joanne told me her daughter had died when she brought over a casserole for me. I was thinking of calling her to see if, by any coincidence, they're Sarah Smith's parents. What do you think?"

"I don't think it could hurt. Maybe this couple was brought into your life for a reason, even though as you said, Smith is a very common name. Go for it, dear."

Kate climbed the stairway to her bedroom, again marvelling at how her life had changed in just a few weeks. Before taking out her cell phone, she prayed they would find someone in Paul's family if it was God's will. It seemed important to him, and the events of the last few weeks helped her to understand how he felt.

"Joanne, how are you?"

"I was just about to dial your number, Kate,"

"Is something wrong at the house?"

"No, everything is perfect. I've got a favour to ask of you. If you are uncomfortable with what I'm asking, please say so. There will be no hard feelings. Two friends of ours, missionaries in Papua New Guinea where we were stationed, are bringing their nineteen-year-old daughter to London to start Western University in September. They want to relocate her now, so she can get accustomed to life here before school starts. She's planning to live in residence. Her parents want to stay close by to support her until she has settled in. They'll be in the London area for six months to a year on furlough from the mission. Fortunately, the mission board has finally realized the need for this, rather than just dropping off your child and going directly back. The culture shock for kids raised on a mission outpost is huge. Our friends knew we were living in the area and called to see if we could recommend a place they could rent. We shared about our difficulty in finding a place. I was wondering if you'd mind if they came to share the house with us. From St. Thomas, it's only a thirty-minute drive to London. They can drive back and forth easily to support their daughter. I didn't suggest this solution to them. I wanted to discuss it with you first."

"Joanne, I'm fine with this arrangement, as I'm fairly sure I won't return to St. Thomas soon. I had a chat with Gran's nurse today. She was away until last weekend. Martha told me Gran has a serious heart condition and could have a heart attack anytime. I plan to spend as much time as I can with her. I'm presently helping her with a charitable trust she is setting up. I also wanted to tell you that Stuart has been arrested after he tried to abduct me. They are taking him back to St. Thomas."

"I saw on the news last night he'd been caught, but they didn't go into much detail. Were you hurt, Kate?"

"No, thank the Lord. Just some bruising. But I was scared. Joanne, there's another reason I'm calling. You mentioned when you delivered the casserole to me that you had a daughter who had passed away. Was her name Sarah?"

"Yes."

"Did she attend McMaster University and die after giving birth to a baby?"

"Yes, how do you know this?"

"My friend Dana has a cousin living on the Island. His parents died last year in a boating accident. He has been sorting through boxes of papers and found an envelope with a locket inside. When he opened it, he saw a picture of a beautiful young woman and strands of her hair. There was a message on the envelope, but no name. McMaster University was stamped on the corner of the envelope. When he showed it to us, we wondered if he was adopted, and his parents never got around to telling him. Gran paid to have a university in the States do DNA testing to see if this woman was his birth mother, and the results showed she was his biological mother. Gran asked Garth Ellsworth, a private investigator, to go to McMaster Hospital and see if anyone recognized the picture of her. An older nurse recalled her giving birth there, but she couldn't remember her name. She told Garth how she had died. He went from there to the Salvation Army Home for Unwed Mothers, and a lady named Josie remembered her name.

"As Gran was sharing all this information with us this morning, an idea was forming in my brain that perhaps you were her parents and Dana's cousin, Paul, is your grandson." Kate could hear crying on the other end, so she said nothing for a few seconds giving Joanne time to digest the news.

"You have no idea what this means to me, and to Don when I tell him. The day we flew back to identify Sarah and make funeral arrangements, the coroner told us she had died from hemorrhaging after childbirth. We were in shock. We had no idea that she was pregnant. If we had known, we would have returned to support Sarah through the ordeal. We asked to see the baby, but it had already been picked up by the adoptive parents and the hospital staff wouldn't tell us their name. We asked who the father was, but no one seemed to know. We had friends in St. Thomas who had an old family burial plot. There was one space they wouldn't be using, so they offered to have Sarah buried there. That is why we retired to St. Thomas. We have a journal she kept from the time she started university, and it shows a picture of an immature young woman in culture shock, with no family around to help her. At that time, the mission boards would not allow a furlough to help your child adapt to a new culture. We shared our story with our mission board, and they finally agreed that going forward, parents could take a six to twelve-month furlough for that purpose. That is why our friends are staying in this area to help their daughter. Kate, tell me about my grandson. We have been saving to hire someone to locate him, but so far we haven't saved enough. I so appreciate your Grandmother's generosity, but we insist on paying her back."

"Your Grandson is Paul Moffet, and he's a chaplain at Nanaimo Hospital on Vancouver Island. Gran shared with us just this morning, while he was here for breakfast, all the information I shared with you. He was relieved to have a name but disappointed that there would be no reunion with his birth mother. I know he'll consider it a wonderful surprise to learn he has two grandparents. By the way, Garth learned Sarah met the adoptive parents a few weeks before giving birth so she could make sure the baby was raised in a Christian home. He's a fine Christian man who is compassionate and caring. He works with mostly dying patients and their families, and he was the one who led my Grandparents to the Lord just a day or so before my Grandfather died."

"Oh, Kate. This is such a blessing. We have prayed for our grandchild and to know where he is and who he is and that he is a Christian is an answer to prayer."

"I want you and Don to talk this over, but I would like to suggest you come here for a visit to get to know your Grandson. We have seven bedrooms, so you are more than welcome to stay here. Gran loves visitors."

"What about Paul's father?" asked Joanne.

"So far, we haven't even got a name. Did Sarah ever mention anyone in her letters or in her journal?"

"Just once. Sarah referred to someone she was dating as Hummer. She said it was a nickname and all his friends called him that. I'll talk to Don about arranging a visit. Thank you so much, Kate."

"God Bless, Joanne. Bye."

chapter seventeen

Kate thought she had probably heard the last from the police but the next night after dinner the buzzer announced someone was at the gate. Officer Hagen said he would like to speak with them for a few minutes. Dana seemed particularly thrilled to hear he was visiting. Since they were just finishing up a delicious lemon pudding, they invited him to join them around the table and insisted on him having a dish.

"This has to be the best lemon pudding I've ever had," Officer Hagen said with a sigh of contentment. "I eat out most of the time and it all starts to taste the same. But I guess I'll keep the economy going."

"You're certainly working late tonight or are you on a different shift?" Dana inquired.

"No, I love my job and I don't mind working after my shift is over. I just thought I'd update you on what we've learned about Stuart and the mystery woman at the airport. Stuart didn't want to answer our questions at first. Then we tried a different approach on the advice of a psychologist who works with the RCMP. She suggested we tell Stuart how impressed we were that he managed to drive from Ontario to Vancouver Island without being pulled over since all the police departments had been given a description of his car and his licence plate number. That worked. Stuart took the bait. With an ego as big as his he had to show us how smart he had been. According to him, he didn't sleep for two days straight and just kept moving west. Then he started resting in his car during the day and travelling at night. When he hit Calgary, he decided to get a wrap put on his car to change the colour from red to blue. Stuart finally spotted a vehicle much like his and stole the licence plates at night so he wouldn't be noticed. As a further precaution, he decided he would try to trade his car for a different one on Vancouver Island. He found an ad for the white sedan in the paper and spoke with the woman who had it up for sale. Stuart used his charm to convince her that she was getting a much better deal by trading her car for his. That was what Stuart shared with us.

"Then, the day after he was arrested, the woman entered the RCMP station at Comox. She had seen on the news that he was arrested, and she was afraid the trade had been part of a scam. She said they agreed to meet at the airport and exchange keys. Stuart was supposed to relinquish his proof of ownership, address and phone number, but as soon as he got the keys to her car, he drove away. She was thrilled with the blue sports car until she saw his picture on the news. We had to take the car from her so our forensic team could inspect it for evidence but she'll get it back. I warned her that Stuart had probably leased his car, so she would have to find out the legal implications of her keeping it. Stuart is undergoing testing in St. Thomas and will then be taken to the Middlesex London Detention Centre to await a court date and trial."

"Another victim of Stuart's charm and schemes," Kate sighed.

"By the way, his fingerprints were all over the knife that forensics found under the driver's seat. It's a good thing you never got in his car, Kate."

"Thank you again for sharing the lemon pudding with me," Officer Hagen said as he picked up his hat. "Dana, there's a rib fest in Chemainus on Sunday. I wondered if you'd be interested in going with me. Starts around seven ."

"I'd love to go. Thanks."

Lily turned to Kate and gave her a wink.

Meanwhile, Kate was feeling rather at loose ends. Paul had moved back home since having a bodyguard on the property was no longer necessary. She assumed he had spoken to Garth by now. Neither Kate nor Lily had told Paul about Kate's phone conversation with Joanne. Until the Smiths called back to tell them how they wanted to connect with Paul, they felt it was better to pray about it and say nothing.

Every Sunday since she arrived on the Island, Lily

and Kate had gone to church at the hospital and listened to Paul preach. Tomorrow was another Lord's Day and Kate looked forward to seeing Paul again. Little by little, she was allowing herself to trust him. From his interaction with her and others, she could honestly say he was sincere, caring and compassionate. Paul had a quiet strength and he certainly didn't appear to manipulate people. She had asked the Lord to guide her relationship with this young man. How she wished she had prayed about dating Stuart. The black and blue marks all over her back were turning yellow, and they were a daily reminder that she should not be wise in her own eyes, but pray about everything.

Vancouver Island is usually blessed all summer with sunny skies, light trade winds and moderate temperatures. Unfortunately, this Lord's Day was an exception. It was unseasonably cool, with high winds and drizzle. As much as Kate was tempted to roll over and enjoy a leisurely Sunday at home, she wanted to see Paul. Dana, Lily and Sandy were already eating breakfast as Kate descended the curved staircase. Dana was looking remarkably perky this morning.

"So, how was the rib fest?"

"Yummy food and great company," Dana said with a grin. "Although I must say, ribs are not the easiest food to eat without getting the sauce all over you."

"He had to find out sooner or later that you're a sloppy eater," Kate teased. "For your next date, you could always buy a snazzy bib."

"We're off for an airshow next Saturday."

"Lily, have you told Garth yet what we found out about Paul's Grandparents?"

"Yes, and I just shared with Dana and Sandy as well. They are all sworn to secrecy until we hear back from Joanne. Garth said he was very impressed with your deductions and thought you might have a career in private investigation."

"Well, if writing children's books doesn't work out, I'll keep it in mind. That reminds me of something. Dana, I have finished proofreading my story. I wondered if we could get together to plan where the illustrations could fit into the text."

"How about this afternoon in the quilting room?"

The ladies arrived a little later than planned at the hospital. The miserable weather had made the roads slippery, so it took considerably longer to make the trip. Paul had just started to lead them in singing. Kate hustled over to the piano and accompanied Paul, who was playing his guitar.

Dana and Lily slipped quietly into two out of three remaining vacant seats at the back of the room. A few minutes later, Dr. McDowell took the third chair. After several short songs were enjoyed by the patients, their families and a few hospital staff, Paul started his sermon.

"I recently had something happen to me that is the

basis for my sermon today. About a year ago, my parents died in a boating accident. I miss them every day, and thank the Lord for the two people who loved me, cared for me and brought me up to love the Lord. I'm convinced I had the best parents in the world. While sorting through the boxes of files and papers they stored in the basement, I came upon this stained, kind of beat-up envelope. Inside the envelope was a tarnished locket. I brought it to show you. When I opened it, there was a picture of a young lady with blond hair. There were also six strands of her hair. Although there were no names on the envelope, the message led me to wonder if I'd been adopted. The answer at the end of the investigation was yes. I was adopted as a baby. At first, I was confused and a little perturbed that my adoptive parents had never shared this with me. Now, I'm counting my blessings. I had a carefree childhood and was loved more than I deserved.

"My friends, this account of what happened to me has a spiritual parallel. God wants to adopt you into his family. We're all his creation, made in the image of God, but we're only adopted into his family if we choose to be. God sent his Son to save you from your sins. When you accept Christ as your Saviour and ask him to forgive your sins, you are born again and adopted into His family. The holy spirit comes to live in you to guide you in living a Christian life and the moment you die, you go to heaven to be with Him. Being adopted into God's family as His child results in his love and blessings being poured out on you. You're never alone again. I guess you could say that I've been adopted twice: first into my earthly family and then into my heavenly family. I'm forever thankful to God for both adoptions. If you haven't accepted Christ as your Saviour, I'd encourage you to do so today. If I can be of any help at all, please contact me. God Bless."

Dana noticed that the middle-aged man sitting next to her suddenly jerked straight up in his chair during Paul's sermon and stared at him as though he was transfixed. Judging by his white coat, she guessed that he worked at the hospital. Before leaving, he approached Paul and they spoke briefly. Kate and Lily then made their way over to Dana, who had just put the song sheets back in the storage cabinet.

"Are you ready to leave?" Kate asked.

"Yes, all tidied up."

"Dr. McDowell, who cared for me when I was stung by the Japanese Wasp, asked to speak with Paul, so he will come to the house when he's finished here."

"He sat next to me, and I thought he looked very perplexed by something Paul said."

"Oh dear, I hope he isn't upset. If he complains about something, they might cancel the Sunday service," Kate said..

"Don't borrow trouble. I'm getting hungry. Let's go," Lily said.

Lunch was interrupted when Kate heard her phone go off. It was an unwritten rule that phones weren't welcome at the table. She quickly checked to see who was calling and when she saw Joanne's name, she excused herself and went out the patio doors.

"Hi, Kate. Don and I have prayed about the best way to enter our Grandson's life. We'd like to take you up on your kind offer to have us stay with you. We feel it would be more comfortable for Paul to get to know us in a familiar setting. If it is inconvenient for you, please don't be afraid to say so. The couple I told you about who have a daughter attending Western University are arriving here today, and they will continue to house-sit for you. Our flight is expected to land at Comox at 4:30 pm tomorrow. A rental car has been booked so we hope to get to your place by 6 pm."

"Everyone here is looking forward to meeting you. I haven't told Paul you have been found. I didn't want to build up his hopes of meeting you if you had decided not to visit. I'll tell him this afternoon. He leads a service at the hospital every Sunday, and I wish you could have heard him today."

"Lord willing, we'll hear him soon." Thank you again, Kate. Who'd have thought that our lives would have intertwined as they have?"

"Goodbye, Joanne."

It was partway through the afternoon when they heard the buzzer, opened the gate and greeted Paul. He quietly ate a sandwich while the others chatted about the service and complimented Paul on his sermon. They were all hoping he would explain why the Doctor asked to speak with him.

When he finished the last bite of his cheese sandwich, he noticed they were staring expectantly at him, so he dropped his bombshell.

"Dr. McDowell is my birth father."

Eyes flew wide open and jaws dropped.

Dana was the first to react. "Kate, didn't you say the man sitting next to me was Dr. McDowell? You mean you've been working in the same place as your Father and you didn't know it? That's bizarre."

"He approached me at the end of the service and requested we meet in the chapel. I had to put the chairs away, but when I got there, it was obvious he was praying and his face was tear-stained. I slipped in beside him so he would sense I'd arrived. He asked if he could see the locket up close. I retrieved it from my pocket, he opened it up and tears started to flow again. Then he told me he'd given Sarah the locket and he was my Father. I was speechless. He asked me where she was living. He had no idea she had died in childbirth. He was distraught when I told him. After he had calmed down, he asked if we could meet tomorrow to talk since he had to go on duty. I invited him to come here for dinner, and I thought we could go down to the beach and talk privately. I hope you don't mind me inviting him without asking you first, but this place has a calming effect on everyone and to be honest, I need your support through this."

"Of course, you were right to invite him here," Lily agreed. "Kate, maybe now would be a good time to share your news."

"We have located your Mother's parents, your

Grandparents. Do you remember me mentioning a retired missionary couple was house-sitting for me while I'm here? Well, their last name is Smith. When she brought a casserole over for me on the day of my parents' funeral, she said she had lost her daughter and she understood how hard it is to deal with grief. I phoned her last night and asked if, by any chance, her daughter was Sarah Smith and if she died after child-birth. They've been praying for you for years and saving to hire a private investigator to try to find you now that they are back in Canada. She phoned me, just before you arrived, to say they are flying in tomorrow afternoon and will be staying here."

"I'm in total awe of God's goodness. Only He could have orchestrated this reunion. I would never have had all these answers to prayer if the three of you hadn't been used by God to make it happen," Paul said.

"I think I'll phone Garth and let him know this investigation is finished. He'll be surprised," Lily chuckled.

chapter eighteen

As Jerry rounded the corner of the house with clippers in his hand, Lily was sitting on the porch waiting for him. "Jerry, I'm so pleased with how you have carried out your duties around the property. Bill appreciates your help and has given me glowing reports."

"Kind of you to say so, Mrs. Grayson. I think this is the best job I've had. I'm considering some horticultural courses at the University of Guelph while I'm there."

"Jerry, we heard back from Mr. Daniels at the car manufacturing company and they are going to supply the materials for building a raised garden at the sight of the accident. They got city approval, have ordered the materials and everything seems to be in place. Instead of working around here next month, I'd like you to be responsible for putting in the garden."

"Sounds like a plan. I could never make up for the hurt I've caused but I think the garden will bring joy."

"I'm pleased to hand your paycheck to you personally this week, and thank you from the bottom of my heart for noticing Stuart's car and calling 911 immediately. Your swift action led to his arrest and stopped a kidnapping from occurring. Kate is very precious to me, and I think it would have killed me if anything happened to her. I've included a bonus with your paycheck. Jerry, you are a fine young man and you remind me of my son, Matt, when he was your age."

"Thank you, Mrs. Grayson, but the bonus wasn't necessary."

"Jerry, the Lord controls my purse strings now, so if you have a problem with the bonus, you'll have to take it up with him. Take care, son."

Lily was thoroughly enjoying helping other people. She wished that instead of driving past churches for all those years, she and Al had stopped, and heard about how God loves and blesses us so we can bless others. If only they had opened the Bibles in their home instead of letting them collect dust. Yes, how different their lives would have been if they had made better choices. Lily couldn't change the past, but she was determined to live a life to please the Lord for whatever time she had left. She was about to sit in her favourite chair to do her devotions when the buzzer rang, indicating someone was at the gate.

Pressing the button, she heard Martha's voice over

the intercom. Moments later, they hugged each other and chatted away like old friends.

"Kate called me and we had a lengthy discussion about me coming here as your companion. Are you sure you want me to move in?"

"I think that would benefit us all. You can have your own room on the second floor, paint in the quilting room or outdoors, have your weekends to roam the Island, and I'll have someone around when Kate is out. She and Paul are going to oversee my Charity Trust, and she'll have to investigate which causes legitimately need help. Also, I want these two young people to have plenty of time to spend with each other."

"Ahh, is a romance blooming there?" Martha asked.

"Things are looking good," Lily said with a grin.

"I'm thrilled to hear this position is available. The apartment I've been renting is a mess with leaking pipes and mould. The landlord could care less. He's renting to people who party all night. It just doesn't feel like home."

"When can you move in?"

"Probably in about two weeks. I can come here immediately to be with you in the afternoons if that works. I'll do my packing in the morning."

"I'm so glad you're coming, Martha."

For the next hour or two, they sat around the kitchen table and discussed the plan in more detail with Sandy, who brought them pieces of freshly baked upside-down pineapple cake and coffee. Lily could remember the days when Al had been at work into the night, and she had spent most days alone. What a blessing that now her house was filling up with friends and visitors.

When the buzzer rang at 3 pm, Kate, who had been working on another children's story, ran to answer the intercom. She was surprised when she heard Joanne's voice, since they didn't expect to arrive until supper. With the change in time, they were earlier than anticipated. Kate took them up the stairs to their room, where they were impressed by the quilt and the amazing view outside the windows. They declined afternoon tea but chose instead to unpack, and then go for a leisurely walk around the property. As Kate was about to leave them, she suddenly remembered she needed to tell them that Paul's Father had been located.

"Paul was late getting here after his service at the hospital yesterday because one of the doctors asked to speak with him. Paul preached on our adoption into God's family, after he told about recently finding out about his adoption as a baby. Then he showed the locket that had been in the envelope he found in a box in his basement. Dr. McDowell, who sat in on the sermon, told Paul that he was his Father, and gave Sarah that necklace. He was extremely upset when he learned of her death after giving birth to Paul. Paul invited him here for dinner tonight so they could share what they know and fill in the blanks. Hopefully, you folks will be able to fill in some as well."

"I brought Sarah's journal with us as it presents a

perfect picture of what she was going through. I wondered if I should share it or not, but after praying about it, I don't think she would mind. Hopefully, that'll bring closure for all of us."

"How did you get her journal, Joanne?"

"After we identified her at the morgue, the coroner handed me a small suitcase she had brought with her to the hospital. Inside were a few pieces of clothing and her journal."

"I'll let you know when Paul arrives. I think he is the finest man that I've met since my Father." Kate said as she left them to unpack.

Joanne and Don exchanged knowing glances. Leaving the bedroom after unpacking, they headed out the patio doors and walked toward the water. Finding the wooden chairs near the cliff, they sat, soaked up the peaceful scene in front of them, and marvelled at the mountains in the distance with their jagged peaks. Holding hands, they prayed that the meeting with their Grandson and his Father would not result in angry words or blame. They knew they were partially to blame for what had happened to their daughter. They only had to read her journal to know how abandoned she had felt. Hopefully, when Paul heard their part in this tragedy, he would forgive them. They asked God to help them connect with Paul and bless this young man who had never known his Mother.

chapter nineteen

Lily rose from her afternoon nap refreshed and intent on calling Garth to tell him the latest news. Within seconds he picked up his phone and Lily filled him in. He explained he had been calling various mission boards to try and locate Sarah's parents but so far had been unsuccessful. He felt they either didn't know the Smiths or didn't want to tell him. Garth was thrilled that the mystery had been solved, and the people involved were about to meet. He liked happy endings and in his business, it wasn't always the case.

He mentioned the possibility of visiting Lily in the near future after he finished one more case requiring his immediate attention. She told him the door would always be open. As she hung up, she thanked the Lord for people like Garth.

Around 4 o'clock, Kate unlocked the gate so it would be wide open when Paul and Dr. McDowell arrived. It wasn't long before she heard a knock on the door, and when she opened it, they were both standing there, having parked their cars in front of the garage. Kate welcomed them and led them outside to the path leading to the cliff. Lily was already sitting with the Smiths and they were hitting it off well. Introductions were made and Kate sensed everyone was somewhat anxious.

"Before we start sharing, I want to pray," Kate said. "Heavenly Father, we thank you for each person gathered here. We believe you have brought us together, and thank you for your unfolding plan for our lives. Help us now to share from our hearts, and show the love that Sarah would want us to show if she could be in our circle today. We thank you for your presence. In Christ's name, Amen."

"Dr. McDowell, perhaps you could tell us how you met Sarah," Kate suggested.

"Please, everyone, call me Bruce. I met Sarah in the university library. It was extremely crowded, and she sat down close to where I was sitting. She looked overwhelmed, so I asked her if she needed help finding the required materials. Sarah indicated she had never used a library like this before, and she had no idea where to start. So I gave her a tour, and helped her locate the materials that she needed. I was also a first-year student, but I had settled in the week before and was paired up with a graduate student who showed me the ropes. Sarah mentioned she had arrived just the day before classes so she had missed out on some information.

"Once she felt more comfortable, Sarah shared about her home in Papua New Guinea and how much she missed her parents. Sarah impressed me as being sweet and kind of shy. She didn't try to flirt and she wasn't loud and rude like many girls. I bumped into her a week later at the bookstore, and I asked her to join me for a coffee at the Campus Coffee Shop. The next day, I took her on a tour of Hamilton. We ended up at Confederation Park.

"Over the next two or three months, we saw each other a lot, going out for coffee, taking long walks and attending events held on campus. I was into photography, so we usually went somewhere with scenic beauty. She tried to share her faith with me, but I felt her beliefs were outdated. I knew this bothered Sarah, so I tried not to put down her religious views. I changed the subject instead.

"Our feelings for each other deepened over the next two months. On one occasion in early November, a friend lent us his car, and we drove north of Campbellville to see the colourful trees. We had no idea where we were going. We just drove around enjoying the countryside and the fall colours. We stopped at a lake surrounded by large evergreen trees. I leaned over to hug her and our feelings and emotions took hold. At one point, she said what we were doing wasn't right. But shortly, things had gone too far. It wasn't planned and yes, we should have stopped.

Instead of being a wonderful experience, Sarah was sad and silent all the way back. From that day on, she wouldn't date me unless we were with other people.

"A few weeks later, while we were in the coffee shop, she told me she was pregnant. I didn't know what to think or how to respond. I was in shock. We walked back to the campus and went our separate ways, agreeing to meet the next day. To me, the solution to our problem was simple. I told her I couldn't take on the responsibility for her and the baby since my parents had a hard time coming up with tuition fees as it was, and I had years of education ahead of me to be a doctor. My future had been carved out. I insisted that the only solution was an abortion. She picked up her books and told me that what she had done was wrong, but she wasn't going to compound the sin by murdering the child she was carrying. I was angry with her for having such outdated ideas. I told her that as much as I loved her, our relationship was over unless she had the abortion. She turned and said good-bye, and that was the last time I saw Sarah. The campus was huge, so it wasn't difficult to get lost in a crowd. I never married because I never found anyone like Sarah. Over the years, I've thought about her and wondered if she got her nursing degree, if the child was a boy or girl, and what the baby was like. Then four years ago, I became a Christian. I know the Lord has forgiven me for my part in Sarah's pregnancy and, ultimately, her death. As I see Paul sitting here today, I thank God for her courage, and I'm so sorry for abandoning her and letting her face the pregnancy alone. I hope Paul, Joanne and Don can also forgive me."

Since all three seemed to be dealing with their emotions, Kate asked Bruce a question.

"How did you become a Christian?"

"A few years ago, I had some holiday time so I contacted my travel agent and wanted to know if any cruises to Alaska were available. She suggested one leaving the next day, the same day as my holidays started. The price was excellent because it was a last-minute seat sale. I didn't know a very popular pastor from a church in California was heading this trip, and the cruise had attracted Christians from all over. I boarded the ship at Victoria and was immediately impressed by the friendliness of the people. It wasn't long before people invited me to the service held each day in a massive room on the ship. At first, I refused because as you know, there are numerous onboard activities you can participate in. But after a few days, I decided to attend a service. God spoke to my heart. The pastor's sermon was on moving past regrets and giving your life to Christ. I invited him into my heart that day and asked him to forgive my sins. I know I'll see Sarah in heaven, but I wish I'd listened to her when she tried to tell me about Christ."

Paul rose from his chair, went over to Bruce and threw his arms around him. Then through their tears, Joanne and Don walked over and it became a group hug.

"Thank you," Bruce said, his voice full of emotion.

Once they were all comfortably seated, Joanne cleared her throat and started sharing about Sarah from their perspective. "Sarah was home-schooled in Papua New Guinea and did very well on the correspondence courses we purchased from Canada. However, she wasn't accepted when she applied to nursing schools much closer to our mission. McMaster was the only one with a good reputation that welcomed her into the program. We contacted our mission board to request a leave of absence or a short furlough to come to Hamilton and support her as she settled in. They refused our request, but said we could accompany her and immediately return. We knew our girl well enough to anticipate she would have culture shock. Sarah had always been shy and hesitant in new situations. Unfortunately, the Mission Board did not authorize us to leave until Sept. 4th, too late for her to take part in the first-year orientation. We saw her to her room the day we arrived, gave her some cash for extras like stamps and personal needs and had to get on the next plane out of Hamilton airport to make our way back to Papua New Guinea. I sensed this was a mistake on our part. We prayed for her constantly, but we felt like we had deserted her, and she was only eighteen years old. Her letters were few and far between. She never spoke of any friends and her news was mainly about the courses she was taking. Sarah never complained, but I could read between the lines that she was unhappy. We hoped her homesickness would lessen as the year went on.

"In March, she wrote in her letter that she wasn't coming home for the summer but would probably get a job in Hamilton to help with expenses for next year. We were genuinely surprised. We took this as a sign that Sarah had adjusted to her new life. Then on August 13th, a call came into the Mission Station that she was dead. We were quite a ways up the river working with a tribe, so it took a day or two before we got the message. They sent in a helicopter to return us to our home base. We had no idea how she had died. People at the mission station had booked us a flight on the first plane back to Canada. We were so distraught that I don't know how we coped with all the plane transfers. When we arrived at McMaster Hospital, we were directed to the morgue, where the coroner had us identify our daughter's body. He gave us a copy of the death certificate and explained that she had hemorrhaged after giving birth. We thought he had confused Sarah with someone else, and we told him our daughter wasn't pregnant. He assured us that she had delivered a baby in the hospital. The coroner handed us a small suitcase containing a few of Sarah's clothes and a journal she had kept since coming to Hamilton. From the morgue, we went to the maternity floor. The staff who were on duty the day she delivered the baby were not available, but they assured us from the records that Sarah had given birth to a baby. Their records indicated Sarah had agreed to adoption, so the adoptive parents were notified and picked up the baby just hours after Sarah died. The head nurse explained they were not at liberty to give the adoptive parents' names or the sex of the child.

"After burying Sarah, we made our return trip home with very heavy hearts, broken by the loss of a daughter we loved so much. For the first time in my life, I was consumed with anger and was mentally making a list of the people I held responsible for losing my daughter: the young man who had made her pregnant, and the mission board who failed to understand how difficult this transition was for missionary children.

"I opened her journal to read on the plane. The last year of her life was very difficult and stressful. She wrote in her first entry that she felt we had abandoned her in a situation she wasn't prepared for. Sarah had no one to confide in, so the journal was an outlet for her feelings. The first several entries explain how difficult simple things like using the laundry room could be. Then the tone of her entry changes a few weeks later. A young man named Hummer (his nickname) helped her get materials that she needed in the library, and judging from other entries, she was seeing him regularly. Then in early November, she writes that she is so disappointed in herself, and feels so much guilt over being intimate with him. She asked God's forgiveness and for His help in not putting herself in such a position again. The following entry is full of anguish. It was confirmed that she was pregnant, and she goes on at length about how disappointed her parents would be if they found out since they taught her that intimacy was for marriage. She knew that from reading her Bible. Sarah blamed herself for this outcome because she had dated someone who wasn't a Christian. The Bible said that Christians should not be yoked with unbelievers. The following entry was about the young man's suggestion that she get an abortion which she refused. She was obviously in love with him but not willing to kill the child inside of her to keep the relationship. The next entry explains her plan. She prayed about keeping the baby or putting it up for adoption and decided that although it would break her heart, she must do what was best for the baby.

"Then in July, Sarah writes about being introduced to a lovely Christian couple who desperately wanted a baby. They lived in Willowdale and after meeting them, she agreed to private adoption. She planned on going back to the home for unwed mothers, where she was staying until university started in the fall. She could continue to work there as a secretary and make a little extra money for school.

"Her final entry is on the morning of the day that she gave birth. It is a prayer for her child to grow up to love the Lord and serve him. She hoped to meet him someday, to know she made the right decision. She ends by saying she will pray for the child and for his father and that both will come to know the Lord.`

"After reading her journal, I knew we were partially to blame for what happened to Sarah. We'd heard of other missionaries who had children that experienced difficulty when they returned to Canada or the United States after being raised on the Mission Field. We should have tried to find a Christian family for her to live with near the university, or since the Mission Board would not give us furlough, we could have left and returned to Canada until she graduated and then reapplied to a Mission Board.

"In hindsight, we made our share of mistakes. But as much as we loved our daughter, she was also responsible for poor choices. She stepped outside the boundaries God set for intimacy and paid the price. We wish she had reached out for help. We would have forgiven her and taken the baby back with us. She could have returned to Papua New Guinea when her courses were finished each year."

"Where is Sarah buried? " Bruce asked.

"I contacted a close friend who used to live in St. Thomas and asked her to pray for us as we returned to claim Sarah's body. She asked us what the burial arrangements were, and I told her we didn't have a plot yet. She offered to have Sarah buried in an extra plot they had available. That's why we retired to St. Thomas just a few months ago. She was our only family and we wanted to be near her."

Lily then filled in bits and pieces of what Garth had unearthed in his investigation. All of their questions were answered, closure had finally come and there was a sense of peace. They realized no one person had been at fault, but it was a combination of wrong choices that ultimately led to Sarah's death. After offering to let Paul and Bruce read Sarah's journal, they all proceeded into the dining room to enjoy a chicken dinner that Sandy had slaved over all afternoon.

When everyone was sitting comfortably in the great room, Lily carried in the quilt top she had been working on. She still had to attach the batting and the back, but the top was all pieced together. She opened it up so only the wrong side of the top could be seen. It had frayed seams, long loose threads, cut-away fabric and even a few blood stains where she had pricked her finger. No one looked impressed with the mess before them.

"What you see here represents what you see when you look back over your life: sin, poor choices, missed opportunities and regrets," explained Lily.

Then she turned over the top of the quilt to reveal how the vibrant greens and rich mauve fabrics created a piece of art that was unique and exquisite. "The right side is what our life will look like from heaven as God shapes each of us into a person of character and a life that reflects his love. God is not finished with us yet. He still has a plan for our life."

As the evening drew to a close, Paul invited his Grandparents and Bruce to come over to his house the next evening for dessert. He told Lily and Kate they were welcome as well, but they both felt that Paul needed some time alone with his new family. Paul gave Lily an extra long hug as the others exited the house, and once again thanked her because none of this would have been possible without the DNA test and getting Garth involved.

A few days later, when Paul came over to pick up his Grandparents for a tour of Chemainus, he had a few minutes alone with Kate on the back patio. They hadn't had hardly a minute alone since Joanne and Don arrived.

"I've some news of my own to share with you," Kate said with a beaming smile. "I've sent my resignation to the Thames Valley School Board and I'm staying here to work on my writing and Gran's charity projects with you. Another missionary couple is living in my house now, and as long as missionaries need a place to stay, I'm okay with that arrangement."

"I've been praying you'd decide to relocate permanently to the Island. I didn't say anything because I wanted you to make your own decision. Kate, you have come to mean so much to me. I want our relationship to deepen as we spend more time together. How do you feel?" asked Paul, moving closer and taking her hand in his.

"I told your Grandparents on the first day they arrived that you are the finest man I've met, except for my Father. I believe God has a plan for our life. We don't know what is just ahead of us or what we'll be doing a decade from now, but the most reassuring reality of being God's child is that He knows. We'll trust him to provide and guide as we seek his will."

Hand in hand, Kate and Paul walked towards an unknown future, secure in God's love and the love that was growing for each other.

sarah's journal

SEPT. 5

I've never kept a journal before but I've never felt as alone as I do at this moment.

Yesterday, my parents left me at the women's residence at McMaster University, to start a four-year nursing program. My Mother handed me this leather-bound journal to record all the wonderful experiences I would have while studying in Canada where I was born but have not lived for the last eighteen years.

From the moment I had to say farewell to our friends at the Mission Station in Papua New Guinea, I felt my anxiety level rise. I was leaving behind everything I held dear, all the familiar faces and a country I loved with all my heart. Of course, I hope to return in four years with my Nursing Degree, and work at the Mission Hospital, or fly out to remote areas to help the people who couldn't get to the station. But right now, four years with no family or friends seems like an eternity. As I write this, my parents are probably on the return leg of their journey back after seeing me safely in my dorm room. The Mission Board said they could not be spared for more than three days, even though my parents explained that getting me settled in this new situation was a priority. I honestly feel totally abandoned.

As soon as they hugged me and left my room last night, I crawled into bed, exhausted from the long trip. I am wide awake now at 6 am. I don't hear anyone stirring on my floor. I'll get dressed, make my way to the bathrooms, and go to the cafeteria. I pray things will go smoothly and this will turn out to be an adventure, not a nightmare.

STILL SEPT. 5 AT 4 PM

My first stop at the bathrooms was a shock. It was an enormous room with several stalls for toilets and showers with only flimsy plastic curtains separating them. A row of sinks was along one wall with no privacy between them. My two worst faults are being sensitive and shy, which made this bathroom challenging to handle. Nevertheless, I quickly used the toilet, washed my face in a sink and left.

Next, I headed for the cafeteria and chose an apple, juice and a muffin. I hadn't eaten since the meal provided on the plane yesterday. When I reached the checkout area, the cashier asked to see my student card. I explained I had just arrived and didn't have a student card. She informed me that *until I had one, I couldn't eat there. The cashier yanked my tray out of my hands and glared at me. Then in a nasty voice, she informed me that if I had registered at Student Registration, I would have a card. I felt like she was accusing me of stealing. Walking down the hall from the cafeteria, I noticed an enormous machine in the hallway. On closer examination, I saw it contained packages of food. I pulled out the Canadian money my parents gave me and purchased two cookies. I munched on these as I headed outside to try to get directions for Student Registration.*

They posted maps of the campus at various locations, so I pinpointed the building I needed and headed in that direction. I was starting to grasp how massive this campus was and the huge number of students attending it. A couple of girls laughed as I passed by and one yelled, "Hey, Frosh, get with it. Lose the dress." I realized that my cotton dress, very comfortable in Papua New Guinea, was not the standard student attire here. Clothes had never been a priority on the mission field. As I glanced around, I saw that most students wore jeans and T-shirts. Nothing in my suitcase even closely resembled their clothes.

I expected a long line at the Student Registration counter, but to my surprise, nobody was ahead of me. A pleasant lady approached and asked me for my documentation. I handed her an envelope from my purse, which contained the paperwork she needed. She filled out a form using information from the sheets in the envelope. Then she turned to me and explained that all the new students had been in a week ago taking part in Frosh Week and an Orientation of the Campus. Now, I knew why I was the only one in line. She said she would have to call a graduate student whose job it was to make Student Cards, so I could use the cafeteria and the library. He arrived in about fifteen minutes, but he looked like he'd been up all night. He grumbled something about people who don't arrive on campus when they should. Apparently, setting up the equipment was not how he envisioned spending his time. He took my picture and within minutes it ejected a card from another machine. I had to sign it and then left, again with glares, even though I apologized for causing him extra work.

After checking with one of the maps again, I walked toward the campus bookstore to purchase the textbooks I would need for my courses. It had just opened, and there were hardly any students inside. They had probably purchased their supplies during Frosh Week. I hunted around but couldn't locate most of the books. Finally, a young woman who worked there approached me and I asked her for assistance. She showed me where they should be found, but indicated that many of them had sold out and were on backorder.

She predicted it would be at least a couple of weeks before they arrived, and suggested that I try to borrow a copy from the library. Great! Another reason I should have arrived at the campus earlier. If only the Mission Board had agreed for my parents to leave earlier, things would have been so much easier.

On the map, the library did not appear to be too far from the bookstore, so I followed the concrete path in that direction. As I looked around, I marvelled at the beautiful buildings, some covered in ivy. I should feel grateful for having this opportunity for an education. But to tell the truth, I felt like a fish out of water and wondered if I belonged here. The library was a huge building with a security guard near the door. I looked for a place to sit but it was really busy, so I approached a table where one seat was still empty. I could feel my heart pumping like I had just run a marathon. Where would I start in this gigantic building full of books to find the ones that I needed? The guy sitting next to me must have noticed my hesitation and bewildered look. He leaned toward me and asked if I needed any help. I took out the list of books that the lady at the bookstore had given me, and explained I had just arrived yesterday and didn't know where to start looking. He seemed surprised that I hadn't been here for Frosh Week and said the orientation involved showing first-year students how to use the library. He told me to follow him and within twenty minutes we had located all the books on the list. When I thanked him for his kindness in helping me, he told me that the name he went by was Hummer.

Tomorrow is Sunday, so I hope to walk around outside of the campus and look for a church.

SEPT. 6

After taking an early shower, to avoid other girls being in the bathroom, I had breakfast and headed out to search for a church. After walking for about fifteen minutes, I came upon a shabby red brick church and followed two older ladies inside. I chose to sit in the back row so I could make a fast getaway if necessary. A few other gray-haired people entered and glanced my way, but none of them spoke.

They sang several songs I was unfamiliar with and then the pastor, an elderly man, preached a sermon on a book he had read that week. I'm so disappointed that no university-age people attended. I had hoped to make some Christian friends, although I have never found it easy to make friends because I'm shy. As the service concluded, people walked past me and no one spoke, so I headed back to the University, having decided to try to find another church for next Sunday. I couldn't help but compare this church to our Mission Church, where everyone was so friendly, the singing was loud and joyful and the message touched your soul.

SEPT 7

This was my first day of classes. I got lost a couple of times but still made it to class on time. In some of my classes, there must be two hundred students. The workload, as outlined by each professor, looks overwhelming. I had hoped to meet a girl who looked like she might need a friend like me, but they have been aloof and unfriendly so far. I think they all found friends during Frosh Week, or they have a roommate to pal with. I'm glad I have a room to myself because there's very little privacy anywhere on campus, and I need a quiet place to study and cry.

I didn't realize how challenging university courses would be, and I don't think I fit in socially. I feel like a fish out of water.

SEPT. 15

I have now been here a week. My classes are interesting, but I disagree with many of the secular views that the professors present. So far, I haven't met any Christians. I have wished many times over the last week that I had the money to buy a plane ticket and go back home. I don't want to disappoint my parents since they saved sacrificially for my education since I was small. I just didn't realize how hard this would be. The other day I went to the laundry room and ran into difficulty again. They had coin-operated washers and dryers, and I had no idea how to use them. I heard snickering from some of the other girls, but eventually, one of the sophomores came over and told me how to work them. Maybe I just have a bad case of homesickness.

SEPT. 16

There was a party in the lounge of our residence tonight. I saw the poster up on the wall and decided to make a real effort to be friendly. I lasted about five minutes. The music was awful, there was a lot of drinking, and the dancing was like nothing I had ever seen before. I returned to my room, finished an essay and then went to bed. I had just gotten to sleep when there was a bang on my door. One of the girls who has the room next door wanted to know if she could sleep on my floor since her roommate had her boyfriend staying the night. I suggested she sleep in the lounge on a sofa where it would be more comfortable. She said that someone would guess what was happening in their room, and her roommate would get into trouble. So I opened the door, and she slept on an air mattress on the floor. She was gone when I woke up in the morning.

SEPT. 17

When I returned to the residence after lunch, the two girls from the room next door were waiting for me outside. They accused me of reporting the girl who had her boyfriend stay all night. I told them I had not told anyone. They didn't believe me and threatened to make my life miserable by telling everyone in the residence that I had squealed on her. I had better get used to being a loner because I'm sure I'll never make friends if they carry out their threat. On days like this, I'm prone to having a pity party and thinking about what I'd be enjoying back in Papua New Guinea. I try to imagine the feel of the tropical sun beating down on me as I collect vegetables from my Mother's small vegetable garden or the fragrant smell of the exotic flowers that are everywhere.

SEPT. 18

I got a letter from Mom and Dad today, and it was so good to hear news from home. I mailed them a letter yesterday, but it *will probably be two weeks before they get it. I only told them about my course assignments because I didn't want them to worry. I tried to think of something else to share with them. The food in the cafeteria is kind of bland and tasteless. I was sure that hearing about the crummy food would bother them, so I couldn't mention that. The one thing that I could share with them is how much I enjoy walking around Cootes Paradise. The stillness and the chirping of all kinds of birds gives me such a peaceful feeling. I'll write about that in my next letter.*

SEPT. 20

Another Sunday has passed without me finding a church. I have continued to walk up and down the streets around the University looking for one. There is a large Catholic Church and a Jewish Synagogue. They are not my faith. I visited the Jewish Synagogue last week because they had a rummage sale. I overheard a couple of girls in the cafeteria talking about the sale. I bought a winter coat, boots, blue jeans and T-shirts. Compared to the prices in stores around here, I got some real deals. I certainly look more like the average university student but my heart isn't here. If I don't feel more at home by Christmas, I'll tell my parents I want to return to Papua New Guinea.

SEPT. 22

I got two of my assignments back today and I did well on them. I stopped at the bookstore to pick up the books on back-

order, and I bumped into Hummer. He wanted to know how things were going and suggested we walk to the Campus Coffee Shop to get a coffee.

He is really easy to talk to and I don't feel shy around him. I shared that I was a Christian. He looked kind of surprised. Apparently, he went to Sunday School when he was young, but he lost interest in religious stuff as he got older. That made me feel sad. He changed the subject.

SEPT. 23

When I returned from my last class this afternoon, Hummer was outside my residence. He suggested taking me on a tour of Hamilton since his friend offered to loan him his car. We ended up at Confederation Park and had the most delicious hot dogs. Today was the best day I have had since I arrived at University. We are going to a football game tomorrow.

OCT. 15

I have been so busy lately that I haven't had time to write in my journal. So far, I have passed all my assignments. I wrote my parents a brief letter and told them about my academic success, and I mentioned I had been on several dates with Hummer. He's been a good friend, taking me places, explaining university procedures, and sharing his hopes and dreams. I really miss not being able to talk about my faith. Every time I bring it up, he changes the subject. I have feelings for him, but it doesn't feel right when he isn't a Christ-

ian. But if I stop seeing him, I don't have anyone else to hang out with.

OCT. 29

We went for a long walk tonight and I enjoyed watching the coloured leaves fall along our path. The whole campus looks like it has been painted, with all the trees ablaze in autumn colours, and it's a magnificent sight. I wish I had a camera so I could share this with my parents.

Hummer took my hand and smiled at me, and I knew right then that he felt the same way as I did. It is so comforting to have someone in my life who cares about me. I feel I can share my feelings with him, and he doesn't judge me. His encouragement in this new situation has meant so much. Hummer suggested we take a little road trip to Crawford Lake in two weeks. I've never been there before and I'm eager to go. John is lending him his car for the day.

When we arrived back at the residence after our walk, he kissed me gently, and I have to say it was the most beautiful experience of my life! He is thoughtful, kind, generous, and as far as I've seen, he doesn't smoke or drink. If only he'd become more interested in having a faith.

NOV. 11

I was so excited as I dressed warmly for our trip to Crawford Lake. Hummer picked me up at 9 am and we drove east and then north until we reached Campbellville. By this time, we were both starving, so we pulled in at a small diner and ordered lunch. We both enjoyed crispy fish and chips. They were extra good because we shared the experience. It wasn't long after that we arrived at Crawford Lake and took a tour of the Iroquois Village that is erected near the lake.

Then we followed the boardwalk around the small tranquil lake, enjoying the smell of fall and the beauty of cascading leaves. By the time we returned to the parking lot, it had completely cleared out except for our car. Hummer leaned over and kissed me, and before we knew it, we were headed down a dangerous path. I was raised to believe that sex outside of marriage was wrong, but how could it be when every part of my being wanted this so much? I knew I should have pulled away and stopped it, but when you want to please someone and enjoy the experience, that is so hard. When we were done, I wished I could say I was still happy, but unfortunately, just the opposite is true. I knew what I had done was not right. I had always pictured my wedding night as special because I had saved myself for the person God brought into my life, and I was committed to for the rest of my life. I had never envisioned it happening in a car parked in an empty lot. All the way home, there was silence. I think Hummer was probably rethinking what we had just done. When we arrived back at the residence, I exited the car as soon as it stopped and ran to the door. What could I say? The day that had started so well had deteriorated because of our poor choices.

NOV. 13

As I was walking toward the lecture hall this morning with the rain pounding down on my umbrella, Hummer caught up to me. He apologized for upsetting me on Saturday and suggested we take things more slowly. I told him that as a Christian, I shouldn't have let it go that far, and from now on, we need to go on dates in a group situation, so there can be no repeats of what happened. He agreed. It was too dreary and wet to stand around talking, so we went our separate ways to our classes. The overcast sky reflected my life.

NOV. 15

I have done a lot of soul-searching in the last couple of days. Sometimes, I think I am so strong and could never give in to temptation like the girls in my residence. But our car trip proves otherwise. Since I arrived in Canada, I haven't been reading my Bible or praying like I used to. I need God's help more than I realized. I plan on doing my devotions first thing in the morning and before bed at night. I knew being intimate with Hummer was wrong on two levels. First, scripture teaches us not to be unequally yoked with unbelievers. So I shouldn't have dated him when I knew he didn't know the Lord. Second, the Bible clearly states that sex outside of marriage is a sin.

At some point, I put what I desired ahead of the boundaries set by the Lord, who I claim to love. I have asked the Lord's forgiveness, and I know from scripture that when we sincerely ask, we are forgiven because of his great love for us.

259

NOV. 17

Hummer and I joined a couple of his friends for bowling last night. It was a lot of fun, and the only physical contact was when he kissed me goodnight. With exams coming in just a couple of weeks, we didn't plan anything because we'll both have to bury our heads in our books. I think the right thing for me to do is to end our relationship after we write our exams. As much as I'm attracted to him, I know this relationship is not pleasing to the Lord. I wish I had handled things better from the beginning.

NOV. 24

I have been studying hard for my exams. The residence has never been so quiet with everyone trying to cram as much into their heads as possible. I woke up today feeling punk, so I skipped breakfast and headed to class. I'm glad it's Friday. I have felt so tired all week that I didn't get much studying done. I hope to catch up on the weekend. I have a few assignments due as well.

NOV. 25

I barely made it to the washroom before I was sick. This is when I miss my Mother. I can't afford to come down with the flu when I have a ton of schoolwork to complete. I decided to go to the infirmary and see if any medicine would make me feel better by Monday.

The nurse at the infirmary was very compassionate. She

took my temperature and did blood work. I didn't have a temperature which we agreed was a positive sign. The results of the blood work will be back on Monday. She recommended I drink lots of liquids until my stomach settled. By the time I left the infirmary, my stomach felt much better, and I was ready to get back to studying.

NOV. 26

It is Sunday and though I planned on taking the bus to visit a church outside the campus, I changed my mind. I felt nauseous again and figured I was not over this bug. It's probably a good idea to rest and work on my assignments.

NOV. 27

I crawled out of bed, and once again, my stomach felt like it would heave. I laid back down for half an hour, climbed out of bed, and got dressed. I visited the infirmary to see if my blood work results were back. The nurse directed me into her office and gave me the news. I'm pregnant. She talked to me about my choices and how to care for myself if I chose to give birth. I don't think I heard a word she said. I was in shock! I skipped my classes, returned to the residence, crawled into bed and cried.

NOV. 28

I haven't seen Hummer in two weeks. Now that classes are back to normal, we meet at the bench outside my residence *when the last class is over. I knew I had to tell him about being pregnant but it was so hard. He looked sad and simply told me that he had to think this over. He said he would meet me back here tomorrow and left. A bad situation is becoming worse, but I know the Lord is with me and I'm not alone.*

NOV. 29

Hummer was waiting when I arrived at our bench. He looked scared and immediately suggested the best way to handle this was for me to have an abortion. He assured me he'd go with me. Hummer explained he was not in a position to accept responsibility for the baby and me since he had eight years of education to finish. He couldn't ask his parents for help because they were sacrificing just to meet his expenses at university.

I gathered up my books and stood up. I told him I would not compound our first mistake by murdering the life inside of me. He became agitated and angry and said we could no longer see each other if I insisted on taking the baby to full term because of some puritanical beliefs. I turned and walked away. God forgives but there are consequences to crossing the boundaries that he puts in place. I prayed for the strength to do this alone.

DEC. 1

I returned to the infirmary to let the nurse know I was not having an abortion. She arranged an appointment with an obstetrician at McMaster Medical Centre. My baby is due in mid-August. I'll probably have to meet with the obstetrician more than once. The nurse also suggested I visit the home for unwed mothers to see how they could help me through this. Fortunately, it is close to the University, so after classes, I walked over there and met with a lady named Josie who oversees the home. She asked about my Christmas holidays and if I was going home. I told her I couldn't because of the distance. She invited me to stay there, and I could do some secretarial work to pay for my room and board. Josie seems to be a joyful Christian. As I was leaving, she gave me a big bear hug and reminded me I was not in this alone. I really needed that hug!

DEC. 20

A Christmas present arrived today from my parents and a letter was enclosed. They are glad I'm passing my exams and can't wait for me to come home this summer. I won't tell them about the baby, at least not yet. I'm praying about whether I should keep the baby or put him or her up for adoption. There is no rush to decide because the birth is still months away. I want the Lord's will in this.

I haven't heard from Hummer or seen him on campus. I spent a few days feeling very angry with him, but as I read God's word, I realized I had to forgive him, just as God has forgiven me. Hummer doesn't know God, so how could I expect him to live by God's commands? I'm praying that someday he will accept the Lord as his Saviour.

JAN. 13

I enjoyed living at the Salvation Army Home over Christmas. I got to know some girls, and Josie was incredibly kind. They have Bible Study each week, and it was almost as good as being back in Papua New Guinea.

Unfortunately, my assignments are getting more difficult. I want to continue to pass so I will have one year behind me. Some girls in my residence are now chatting with me in the laundry room or cafeteria, but none seem interested in really being my friend. I haven't told anyone here that I am pregnant. How can I witness to them about the Lord when I made such a colossal mistake? God has forgiven me, but I don't know if I'll ever forgive myself.

MARCH 20

The school year is almost over. My parents expect me to fly back home in a few more weeks. I'm going to the Salvation Army Home to see when I could return there. Usually, the girls arrive about a month before their delivery date.

I saw Hummer in the distance today, laughing with a group of students. He seems to have gone on with his life, and I guess I'm just a fleeting memory. It seems unfair that the guy is free to live with no responsibility while the girl pays the price in more ways than one. Again, I felt some bitterness, so I prayed and asked God to give me a heart of love. A guy in my psychology class asked me out to a movie. I could tell by the title of the film that he wasn't a Christian, so I declined. I can't believe I haven't met a

Christian on campus. Don't Christians go to University in Canada?

APRIL 3

Josie, at The Salvation Army Home, assured me I was welcome to come and stay there in return for my help at the front desk and doing some routine secretarial work. I thanked the Lord for this answer to prayer. I wrote to my parents and told them I had work here and would not be coming home this summer. I know they will be disappointed, but I'm trying to spare them worry, and I would rather that they don't know I'm pregnant until I've figured out what is best for the baby.

MAY 22

I'm once again enjoying my stay at the Salvation Army Home. My secretarial jobs keep me busy, and they have given me more responsibility as I prove myself. I received a letter from my parents, and although they are disappointed I'm not coming home, they are thankful that I feel so much at home in Canada. In some ways, I feel like I'm deceiving them. Until now, I've always been honest with them. I don't think they would guess I was pregnant, not in their wildest dreams. Just looking at me, you can't tell I'm pregnant. I have always been thin, and I was so nauseous for the first three months that I lost weight instead of gaining any. I go to see the doctor for a check-up in six weeks. At my last appointment, they told me they could reveal the sex of the child if I wanted to know. I told them I would rather wait until this baby was born.

JULY 9

The doctor seems to feel that everything is moving along with the pregnancy, just as it should. I mentioned I seemed to tire quickly but he didn't comment. They did more blood work while I was there and said they would contact me if there was a problem. I've got a round tummy now, and I can feel the baby moving. I've another appointment in early August, about two weeks before the baby is due.

A Salvation Army Captain came today to lead our Bible Study. He asked for prayer for a Christian couple who have been trying to have a baby for a few years. Each time the wife miscarriages, they are devastated. Now, they are trying to adopt. When the meeting was over, I went up and spoke with him. I told him I was still praying about keeping my baby or putting it up for adoption. I asked him if this couple would consider coming to Hamilton so we could meet. He arranged the meeting and I was impressed with them. They are very much in love, and they explained how hard they tried to have a child, and how long they had prayed for one. I sensed their strong desire to provide a Christian home for a baby.

I knew immediately that this was the right home for my baby. I want this child to have a Mother and Father and have a wonderful childhood like I did. The adoption is a private adoption involving an attorney that did legal work for the Salvation Army. The hospital will call them as soon as I deliver the baby and they will pick him or her up to take home. I'm at peace with this decision.

AUGUST 1

I was supposed to see the obstetrician today, but I was so tired I decided to stay put. As far as I know, there was no problem with the blood work from my last visit, so I will just rest. Josie insisted I stop working for the next two weeks and get more rest. I'm going to pack a suitcase to take to the hospital when it is time. Then I'll crawl back into bed and sleep. I'm starting to be anxious about the delivery and have wondered if I'll have the courage to hand over this baby after seeing him or her. I don't have the energy to write more in my journal today.

AUGUST 13

I woke up to a very wet bed. I think my water must have broken. I'm having weak contractions but nothing terrible so far. I need to get dressed, order a taxi and grab my suitcase before I leave for the hospital. It could be hours before I deliver this baby, but I don't want to take any chances. Usually, Josie accompanies a girl in labour, but she was driving all the girls early this morning to Niagara Falls for the day.

Last night, I took the time to write a short note to my baby and put it in a brown envelope with the locket Hummer gave me, containing my picture and a piece of my hair. I want my baby to know I love him or her. I continue to pray for Hummer and this unborn child that they will feel God's love and delight in doing his will. How I wish I had a loving husband driving me to the hospital, going through the birthing process at my side and then celebrating with him the birth of our first child.

Things could have been so much different if I had obeyed God's word and not made the wrong choices. Yet, I know that God never forsakes his child, and he will be with me. I hope to meet this child someday and know I made the right decision. If I don't ever meet the baby or Hummer again on this earth, I pray that they will accept Christ as their Saviour and I'll see them in heaven.

note to readers

Dear Readers,

Thank you for joining Kate as she experiences life as a young woman with all the challenges and decisions that she has to make. It is a period in her life where unwise choices can have consequences that she doesn't fully understand. Kate, fortunately, got sound advice from her parents, in the letter they left her, and also from Joanne, a mature woman. More importantly, as she searched God's word and prayed, she walked more closely with God and obtained wisdom.

The world we live in defines success by our ability to accumulate money and social status. It can become an idol that takes the place of God, as it did for Al and Lily. God's definition of success is very different and as you read the Bible, you will better understand what real success is all about.

Loss and grief are, unfortunately, a part of everyone's life. Several characters in this novel faced a tragic personal loss. Christians are blessed to have the hope of seeing their loved ones again in heaven. They also have the Lord to walk with them as they try to adjust to life without someone they love. The Lord often brings people into their lives, like Joanne and Don Smith, to encourage and offer practical support as they deal with their grief.

God has a one-of-a-kind plan for each of our lives. Through prayer and Bible reading, we can get the wisdom and understanding we need to follow His unfolding plan. If you have never given your heart to the Lord, I would like to encourage you to bow your head, ask Him to forgive your sins, and invite Him to be your Savior. He came to this earth, was crucified and rose again to make this possible. He wants a close relationship with you.

I love to hear from my readers, and it is my prayer that something in this story has touched your heart. My e-mail address is webstereva@rogers.com.

God Bless you and keep you.

Eva

discussion questions

1. Grief is often an all-consuming emotion that can distort how we view our life. How did grief affect Kate negatively?
2. Kate had a plan for her summer. But it was shattered by the death of her parents? How much control do you think you have over the direction your life takes? Should you make plans or just fly by the seat of your pants?
3. Kate's parents never told Kate what they thought of Stuart. Why do you think they didn't do so? What do you think they thought of Stuart?
4. What were some red flags in Stuart's behaviour? Why do you think she didn't see these earlier?
5. Kate felt her church had not accepted or supported her. Do you think this was her

fault or is there any evidence the church she attended was not following scripture concerning how brothers and sisters in Christ treat each other? What advice would you give her church on how to care for the body of Christ?

6. Anger, bitterness and unforgiveness seem to be close relatives. Who was instrumental in helping Kate see the connection between these? If Kate had refused to forgive her Grandmother and stayed in St. Thomas for the summer, how would other characters' lives, as well as her own, have been affected?

7. Lily was submissive to her husband when he made it clear that they were not to have contact with Matt until he returned to take over the business. In your opinion, was she right or wrong?

8. What did Al's stubbornness, bitterness and unforgiveness cost them?

9. What evidence do you see in Lily's life to show that she has genuinely given her heart to the Lord?

10. Money can be a blessing and a curse. Discuss what effect having it or not having it had on the characters in this story.

11. Paul's parents chose not to tell him he was adopted. Do you agree or disagree with their decision?

12. Why do you think Sarah was intimate with Bruce when she clearly knew it went against God's word? What are some suggestions you would have given her to avoid this happening?

13. Even though Sarah sinned, how do you know she is a Christian?

14. Sarah decided to put her baby up for adoption and not tell her parents she was pregnant. Do you agree or disagree with her choices?

15. Creativity is a beautiful gift from God. Discuss how the following characters were using their creativity: Kate, Dana, Paul, Lily, Sandy, Martha, and Bruce.

16. Paul and Kate both have reasons for not getting romantically involved. Do you think they are valid?

17. Lily played a role in match-making between Paul and Kate. Discuss what she did to encourage the relationship.

18. Jerry was driving the truck that killed Kate's parents. Do you find it hard to believe that Kate and Lily would forgive him? What were the positive results of their forgiveness?

19. Sometimes, a seemingly minor decision can have enormous consequences for good or bad. Think about the characters in this story. Who can you identify as making a small

decision but there was an unexpected outcome?

20. There is an old saying, 'Prayer changes things.' How were some characters' lives or situations changed by prayer?

bible verses

Bible Verses related to the Principles and Morals this story is based on.

Sorrow – Revelation 21: 4-8

Feeling Alone – Deuteronomy 31: 8

Anger – Ephesians 4: 26-27

Disappointment – Psalm 22: 4-5

Guidance – Psalm 25: 12

Forgiveness – Hebrews 12: 14-15

Ephesians 4:31-32

Unbelievers – 2 Corinthians 6: 14-18

Sexual Purity – Hebrews 13: 4

1 Timothy 4: 12

Salvation – John 3: 16

Money – 1 Timothy 6: 6-10

Matthew 25: 33-40

Unborn Baby – Psalm 139: 13-16

recipes

JOANNE'S HAWAIIAN BEAN CASSEROLE

Joanne often makes this casserole for herself and Don. She also prepares it for church potlucks because it is easy and inexpensive.

Sweet onions (chopped), 1 cup

Cooking oil, 1 tablespoon

Bacon (chopped), 4 slices

Red kidney beans, 19 oz can

Browned beans in tomato sauce, 14 oz. can

Crushed Pineapple, 1 cup

Ketchup, $\frac{1}{3}$ cup

Prepared mustard, 1 $\frac{1}{2}$ teaspoon

Brown sugar (packed), $\frac{1}{3}$ cup

Worcestershire sauce, $\frac{1}{2}$ teaspoon

Pepper, $\frac{1}{8}$ teaspoon

Heat the oil up in a pan and add the onions and

bacon to fry until the onions are soft and the bacon is cooked. Put into a 1 ½ quart casserole. Then add the remaining ingredients. Stir to mix it well. Bake uncovered in a 350-degree oven for 1 hour until it bubbles. Joanne always stirs it a couple of times while baking.

Great with a tossed salad and cheese scones.

CHEESE SCONES

1 ¾ cups all-purpose flour

2 tablespoons sugar

2 tsp baking powder

½ tsp salt

¼ tsp baking soda

⅓ cup cold butter

1 cup buttermilk

1 cup plus two tablespoons grated old cheddar cheese

Combine the first five ingredients in a bowl and cut in the butter until the mixture resembles coarse crumbs. Or if you have a food processor, you can put the first five ingredients in that and use it to cut up the butter by hitting it briefly. If you use the food processor, transfer the mixture to a bowl and stir in the buttermilk just until blended. Gently fold in the 1 cup of grated cheddar cheese. Turn out onto a floured surface and knead about seven times. Pat into a 9-inch circle. Cut into eight wedges. Separate wedges and place them on a greased baking sheet. Sprinkle the two tablespoons of grated cheese over the top of the scones.

Bake at 450 degrees for 12 minutes or until golden brown. Cool a bit on a rack. Joanne and Don like them warm.

ADA'S BUTTER TARTS

Sandy's close friend Ada shared this recipe with her thirty years ago. It's a keeper.

Pastry:

2 ¼ cups all-purpose flour

1 tablespoon brown sugar

½ teaspoon salt

½ cup butter, keep it cold and cut into cubes

½ cup shortening, keep it cold and cut into cubes

6 tablespoons ice water, enough to bring it together

Using a food processor, pulse the cold butter and shortening into the flour, sugar and salt until it is the size of peas. Dump into a bowl.

Sprinkle water over the surface and toss with a fork until the water is mixed into the dough. Handle the dough as little as possible.

Form the dough into two disks about an inch thick. Wrap in plastic wrap and leave in the fridge for half an hour.

Roll out on a lightly floured surface. Cut into circles with a 4-inch cutter. Fit into muffin cups or tart tins. Put into the fridge until you have the filling prepared.

Filling:

2 eggs

1 cup brown sugar (packed)

½ cup corn syrup

1 tablespoon vinegar or lemon juice

1 teaspoon vanilla

½ cup butter, melted

Raisin, nuts or coconut

Heat oven to 425 degrees.

Beat eggs slightly, then beat in sugar, syrup, lemon juice, vanilla and butter.

Put a few raisins, chopped pecans or coconut in the bottom of each tart.

Fill tart shells two-thirds full with the liquid mixture. Not to the top or they will boil over the top and you will have a hard time getting them out of the tins.

Back 15-20 minutes in the bottom rack of the oven.

Let them sit for 5 - 10 minutes before you try to remove them from the tins.

Lovely with a side of ice cream.

SANDY'S LEMON COOKIES

This cookie dough needs to be refrigerated for 2 hours before baking.

1 cup butter, softened

2 cups sugar

2 large eggs, room temperature

2 teaspoons grated lemon zest

3 tablespoons lemon juice

2 ¾ cups all-purpose flour

1 cup quick-cooking oats

2 teaspoons baking powder

¼ teaspoon salt

Extra sugar

Directions:

In a small bowl, combine the lemon zest and the sugar and mix thoroughly. Set aside.

In a large bowl, cream butter and add sugar and lemon zest. Beat in eggs and lemon juice.

In another bowl, whisk flour, oats, baking powder and salt; gradually beat into creamed mixture. Refrigerate covered for 2 hours or until firm enough to shape.

Preheat oven to 375 degrees. Shape level tablespoons of dough into balls and roll in the extra sugar. Place 2 inches apart on parchment-lined baking sheets. Flatten slightly with the bottom of a glass.

Bake until edges are light brown, approx. 7 minutes. Remove from pans to wire racks to cool.

SANDY'S APPLE SQUARES

2 ¼ cups flour

¾ cup dark brown sugar

1 cup butter, melted

½ cup quick (not instant) rolled oats

6 apples, peeled and chopped

¾ cup white sugar

1 teaspoon vanilla extract

½ teaspoon cinnamon

1 cup cold water

Preheat the oven to 350 degrees. Grease a 13 x 9 in. baking pan. In a medium bowl, combine 2 cups flour, brown sugar, butter and oats. Reserve 1 cup of the oat mixture; set aside. Press the remaining oat mixture into the prepared pan and put in the oven for 5 minutes to set the bottom crust. When you remove it from the oven, spread the apples over the crust.

In a medium saucepan, combine the brown sugar, vanilla, cinnamon, remaining ¼ cup of flour and 1 cup of water until well combined. Cook over medium-low heat until thick, stirring often. Pour over the apples. Sprinkle the top with reserved oat mixture. Bake until golden brown, about 40-45 minutes. Cool completely on a wire rack before cutting into squares or bars.

Sandy likes to serve these for dessert with a scoop of caramel ice cream or whipped cream.